ANIMORPHS

The Forgotten

K.A. Applegate

GRACEMOUNT HIGH SCHOOL LIBRARY

17479

7/99

Hippo

For Michael

Scholastic Children's Books,
Commonwealth House, 1 – 19 New Oxford Street, London WC1A 1NU, UK
a division of Scholastic Ltd
London ~ New York ~ Toronto ~ Sydney ~ Auckland

First published in the USA by Scholastic Inc., 1997
First published in the UK by Scholastic Ltd, 1998

Copyright © Katherine Applegate, 1997
ANIMORPHS is a trademark of Scholastic Inc.

ISBN 0 590 11256 2

All rights reserved

Printed by Cox & Wyman Ltd, Reading, Berks.

10 9 8 7 6 5 4 3 2 1

This book is sold subject to the condition that it shall not, by way of trade or
otherwise, be lent, resold, hired out, or otherwise circulated without the
publisher's prior consent in any form of binding or cover other than that in
which it is published and without a similar condition, including this
condition, being imposed upon the subsequent purchaser.

Chapter 1

1:22 P.M.

My name is Jake.

I can't tell you my last name, or where I'm from. That would just help the Yeerks. They'd love to find me and my friends. They'd love to know who we are, even *what* we are.

Knowing my last name isn't important for you. What you need to know is that everything I'll tell you here is true. It's real. It's actually happening. Right now.

The Yeerks are among us.

The Yeerks *are* us.

They're a parasitic species. They live inside the bodies of other beings. They take over your mind and body.

Controllers. That's what you call a creature that is ruled by a Yeerk. A Controller. Something

1

that looks human, acts human, sounds human, but whose mind is Yeerk.

They are everywhere. They can be anyone. Think of the one person in the whole world that you trust the most. Think of that one special person. And now realize, *believe*, accept the fact that they might not be the person you think they are. Deal with the reality that behind those friendly, loving eyes lives a grey slug.

That's what a Yeerk looks like in its natural state. Just a grey slug. They enter your head, squeezing through the ear canal, and flatten themselves out to envelop your brain.

You know all those nooks and crannies in brains? You've probably seen pictures in school. Well, the Yeerk forms itself into those nooks and crannies and it ties into your mind.

You wake up and you want to scream, but you can't. You can't scream. You can't move your eyes or raise your finger or make yourself walk. The Yeerk controls you.

You're still alive. You can still see what's happening. Your eyes move and focus, but you're not moving them. You can still hear your own mouth speaking and using your voice. You can feel it when the Yeerk opens up your memories and looks through them. You can hear the Yeerk laughing at you as it pries into your every secret.

I know. Been there. For a few days, I was a Controller.

The Yeerks are here, all right. Their mother ship is parked in high orbit right now. It's hidden from human radar, but it's there.

And the Yeerk super-evil leader, Visser Three, is there, too.

We are being invaded. We are being enslaved. We are losing our own planet. And we don't even know it.

My friends and I fight the Yeerks. But we're just five kids. Well, five kids and one Andalite. Yes, we have some amazing powers, but we're still desperately weak and outnumbered compared to the force of the Yeerk invasion.

We are the only humans resisting the Yeerks.

We may be the only hope that Earth has.

We have a lot on our shoulders.

Which is why I really, really, *really* did not see why I had to have more suffering piled on.

Wasn't I under enough stress? Life wasn't bad enough? We had to have . . . square dancing?

Square dancing! The horror!

The CD player was blasting out screaming-cat fiddle music. Which, in my opinion, is possibly the worst music ever created.

The lights in the classroom seemed blazingly bright compared to the dark grey clouds outside. The teacher was standing off to the side. She was wearing that smug, satisfied look teachers sometimes get when they know they are grinding the students' last nerves.

3

"Now promenade left! Bow to your partner, do-si-do!" the stereo drill-instructor yelled.

I promenaded, which consists of walking like a BIG HONKING GOOBER around in a circle.

And then I bowed. A strange, jerky sort of movement.

And finally, my least favourite thing: I did a do-si-do. Or as the shrieking, yammering voice on the CD said, do-si-DOOOO!

"You call that do-si-do?" Rachel sneered as I high-stepped backwards around her.

"Don't mess with me, Rachel," I warned.

"Smile, Jake. Big smile!" Rachel said. "We are happy while dancing. Happy!" She was so totally enjoying torturing me.

Rachel is my cousin. She's an Animorph, too.

"Now swing your partner back to the left and promenade!"

"Promenade this," I muttered darkly.

I grabbed Rachel to swing her. I was considering swinging her into the nearest wall. But although Rachel may look like some dippy *Clueless* type, she's a lot closer to being *Xena: Warrior Princess*.

In other words, I'm just a little scared of Rachel. I've seen her in lots of battles. You just really don't want to make her too mad. You really, *really* don't.

"Excellent swing," Rachel mocked me. "Now

you're getting into it. I can just picture you in a string tie, cowboy boots, maybe a bright red-checked western shirt—"

"Don't push it, Rachel," I warned again.

Then the worst possible thing happened. As I was "promenading" yet again, I heard Rachel yell.

"Hey, Cassie! Come by to watch?!"

My heart sank. Cassie is another member of our team. She's also someone I really kind of like. If you know what I mean. And I really didn't want her watching me as I stomped clumsily around the circle.

The sight of me, big old Jake, galumphing around in time to fiddle music was guaranteed to destroy any affection Cassie had for me. I mean, I was making *myself* sick. I could just imagine how I looked to Cassie.

I met Cassie's gaze. She was standing in the doorway of the classroom. And she was laughing. She was laughing with her entire body. She was in convulsions.

I was so relieved. See, I was afraid I'd get a pitying look.

Instead, she was cracking up. Tears were rolling down her cheeks as I "do-si-doed" right in front of her.

"You find this funny? Me, trying to dance?"

Cassie couldn't talk. She was laughing too hard. She just nodded.

What could I do? I started laughing, too. There wasn't anything else to do.

Oh, maybe one other thing. I grabbed Cassie's hands and pulled her into the circle. Rachel backed away, letting Cassie take her place in the pattern.

Cassie stopped laughing.

"No way!" she said, alarmed.

"Let's see *you* do-si-do," I said.

I grabbed her and swung her, and in a breathless voice she whispered, "I just came by to tell you something. Tobias wants us. Right after school lets out. It's something big."

I took a deep breath. Suddenly, I wasn't in the mood to laugh any more. Tobias wouldn't say "something big" unless it was something big.

And "something big" meant something bad these days.

Cassie and I had to obey the music and separate then, but a few seconds later, we rejoined in the pattern, bowing to each other.

"I guess square dancing doesn't seem so bad now, huh?" Cassie asked me.

"Yeah, right. It would take more than the danger of sudden death to make square dancing OK," I said. "A lot more."

I did some more promenading. I did some more bowing. I did some more do-si-doing.

But my thoughts were already running ahead, wondering what Tobias had seen. And just how much of a mess it would end up being.

Then. . .

FLASH!

I fell!

I fell down and down through the green, green trees!

A branch. I snatched at it with my hand and swung and released, then flew through the air and caught another branch. I wrapped my tail around the branch and turned to look back. Monkeys were swinging towards me through the high tree-tops of the jungle.

I was giddy.

It was a rush!

It was. . .

FLASH!

Cassie was smiling, and looking a little strangely at me. The music was done. The class was breaking up.

"Are you OK?" Cassie asked me.

"Yeah. Yeah," I said, shaking off the weird vision.

"Daydreaming?" Cassie asked me.

"I guess so," I said.

"I wonder what Tobias wants. Do you have any idea?"

I was too confused to really respond. One second I'd been square dancing. The next second I'd been swinging through the trees.

And both moments had been real.

7

Chapter 2

3:08 P.M.

"**W**hat do you think?" Marco asked me. "Personally, I figure Tobias found some really good road-kill, and he wants us to share."

"Yeah, that's probably it," I said tolerantly. Marco's approach to everything is to joke about it. Especially when he's worried.

After school we all went our separate ways. Cassie to her home, Rachel to hers. We all knew Tobias had some serious reason to talk to us. We were all afraid it was trouble of some kind.

But I had something extra to worry about. The hallucination, or vision, or whatever it was I'd had was too real to just forget. Everyone day-dreams. This was no day-dream. I was in the jungle. Period. It was for just a few seconds, but it was definitely real.

But like I said, priority number one was figuring out what was bugging Tobias. So Marco and I walked home together because that's what we usually did. And it is very important for us to act normal. We don't want to draw attention. So we try and be like we always were. Like we were before the night that changed our lives for ever.

We'd been walking home from the shopping mall at night. We took a shortcut through an abandoned construction site. A really stupid, irresponsible thing to do. But it turned out it wasn't axe murderers or kidnappers we had to worry about.

Before that night we'd all known each other, but we weren't a group. We had just happened to hook up at the mall. It was an accident or fate or something. Take your pick.

Anyway, the five of us ended up walking together as we were leaving the mall. And in a dark, spooky construction site, with empty, half-finished buildings all around us, we saw the spaceship land.

It was an Andalite fighter. It was badly damaged. Up in orbit, the Andalites had come out on the wrong end of a fight with the Yeerks.

The Andalite pilot of the fighter was named Elfangor. Prince Elfangor. He was dying. He was the one who told us about the Yeerks.

Life changed that night. Life went from being just the daily stuff any normal kid has to

9

deal with, to knowing a secret that made you want to sit down and cry.

It was Prince Elfangor who gave us the power to morph. It was all he could do to help us. It was the only weapon he could give us.

The power to morph. To *become* any animal we could touch and "acquire".

A great and awful power. A power that has given me some serious nightmares.

I've seen things since that night at the construction site. Things I wish I'd never seen. And I've done things I wish I couldn't remember.

"Hey," Marco said, interrupting my thoughts. "Speaking of Bird-boy. Up there. Is that anyone we know?"

I followed the direction he was looking. It was a dark afternoon and the sky just kept getting darker. It was filling up with rain clouds the colour of steel wool. And there, silhouetted against the clouds, was a large bird.

Even from a distance you could tell it was a bird of prey.

"Could be. I can't tell," I said. "If it's Tobias he'll spot us."

Tobias is in hawk morph. Permanently. See, there's a nasty little hook buried inside the morphing power: stay in morph for more than two hours, and you stay in morph for ever.

Tobias has the soul and mind of a human. But his body is the body of a red-tailed hawk.

"He's coming closer," Marco said.

"Yeah." I had mixed feelings. Tobias is one of us. A friend. More than a friend. He's risked his life for me many times. But I sensed he was bringing bad news. And I really didn't want to hear bad news.

I heard his thought-speak voice in my head.

<Jake. Marco.>

"See? Figured it was him," Marco said.

We couldn't answer Tobias. He was still too high up to hear us speak, even with his excellent hawk hearing. And you can only make thought-speak when you're in morph. Or if you happen to be an Andalite.

<You guys need to move it a little faster,> Tobias said. He sounded tense, impatient, excited. Not that he really "sounded" at all. But his thought-speak in my head carried tension. <Morph as soon as you get a chance, OK?>

I looked at Marco. He sighed.

"My dad should still be at work. We can use my house," he said. "We're almost there."

We headed straight for Marco's house. We live in the same district, just a couple of blocks away from each other. Most of the kids in our school live there, including Rachel. Cassie lives out on her farm a little way down the road.

<I'll round up the others,> Tobias said. <We'll meet up with Ax later. I'll catch up with you once you get airborne.>

11

"This has 'big trouble' written all over it," I muttered.

"In huge red neon letters," Marco agreed.

We reached Marco's house and went in. Marco checked to make sure we were alone.

"Dad! Dad, you home? Any one home? Hey, Dad, I'm going to change all the settings on your stereo!" Marco winked at me. "If he's home, that'll make him come running."

There was no reply. Just a quiet house.

We ran up the carpeted stairs to Marco's room. We ran past framed pictures of Marco and his dad and his mother, who everyone thought was dead.

Marco opened his bedroom window as wide as it would go. The breeze was cool and damp. It was going to rain. And I hate rain.

"Let's get this over with," I said. I kicked off my shoes and removed everything but my morphing suit. Marco did the same.

I focused my mind on a bird. It was a peregrine falcon. The DNA of that falcon was part of me. And, thanks to the Andalite morphing technology, I could trade that DNA for my own.

I focused my mind and the change began.

Feather patterns appeared on my skin as if some invisible person had drawn them there.

The not-terribly-clean floor of Marco's room came rushing up at me as I shrank, dwindling down like a fast-burning candle. It was like

12

falling and falling without ever quite hitting the ground.

Or in this case, hitting a dirty white sock.

"Oh, man," I said. "Marco, you could at least not leave dirty gym socks around."

"Hey, I've seen your room," Marco said. "You still have some of your old nappies lying around."

He started to say more, but that's when his human tongue shrivelled down to become a tiny bird tongue. So all he said was "Craww hee hrrar."

Whatever that meant.

The dirty gym sock went from being the size of a sock to being the size of a blanket. The only good thing was that falcons don't have much of a sense of smell. I was grateful for that.

My lips became hard as fingernails and began to press outward, forming a sharp, down-curved beak. It was weird and disturbing because I could actually see the beak grow, like some humongous nose.

My feet were gone, replaced by talons that could open up a prey animal like a can-opener on a can of cat food.

My bones made grinding, squishy noises as my skull shrank. My arm bones became hollow and other bones disappeared altogether.

Then the patterns of feathers on my skin grew three-dimensional. It was eerie to watch — like my skin was chapping really badly. Like skin

13

was peeling up at an incredible rate, and each peel of skin formed a feather.

Grey feathers, mostly.

I glared at Marco with my incredible Force-10 falcon vision.

He glared back with the eyes of an osprey.

<Let's catch some air,> I said.

I flapped my wings twice and hopped up to the window-sill.

<Last time I was in osprey morph some peregrine took a shot at me,> Marco said. He sounded a little resentful. Like it was my fault. He hopped up to the sill beside me.

<Don't worry, Marco. I'll protect you.> I said it knowing it would make him mad.

<Protect me? Right. Come on, big guy, let's fly. See if you can keep up with me first. Then see if you can "protect" me. Hah!>

I opened my wings wide, kicked off from the window-sill, and dropped straight for the grass in Marco's backyard.

This is always terrifying. See, you know you're a bird and all, but in your mind you're still a human. And jumping out of windows scares humans. I was three or four metres off the ground, with nothing but lawn to catch me if for some reason my wings didn't work.

But then my wings caught the air. I felt the pressure of the air pushing up beneath me. I flapped hard, one, two, three, four, and shot forward. Forward and upward.

I flapped and flapped, working hard to get altitude in the cool air. Flapping is hard. Just because you're a bird doesn't mean flapping is easy.

Marco and I had just managed to climb maybe fifteen metres when Tobias came zooming up alongside us, zipping around like he'd been born a bird.

<Follow me,> he said.

<Follow you where?> I asked, maybe a little too grouchily.

Tobias laughed. <We're going to the supermarket,> he said. <We're going to the Safeway.>

<Tobias, are you nuts?> Marco demanded. <The supermarket? What, is there a sale on gourmet birdseed?>

<Funny, Marco,> Tobias said. <But it's not about birdseed. This supermarket seems to be having a sale on high-ranking Controllers.>

Chapter 3

It's hard to be worried when you're flying.

You feel so powerful, floating high above the heads of all the little people below you. People are so slow. They walk in little lines along pavements, always stuck moving in two dimensions: left-right, forward-back.

A bird moves in three dimensions and has a lot more going on when he's flying. There's the air temperature, the speed of wind gusts, the steadiness of the breeze — crosswinds and thermals and humidity.

Your wings and tail are constantly adjusting — extending your wing tips, spreading or narrowing your tail, altering the angle of attack.

Fortunately, the falcon's brain handles all of that. Because let's face it, as a human, I know

16

basically nothing about flying.

All I know is it's the coolest thing in the entire world.

Marco and I flew along with Tobias till we spotted two other big birds of prey rising up towards us: Rachel and Cassie.

<Break it up a little,> Tobias advised. <We're going to draw every bird-watcher within a hundred kilometres. Spread out. Stop thinking like humans — we don't have to be bunched together to see the same things.>

He was right. Falcons, hawks and eagles don't exactly fly in flocks together. And with the intense vision of our bird morphs, we could see whatever we were supposed to see from half a kilometre away.

I wanted to get altitude because I was struggling with the dead air around me. I had the narrowest wings of the group. I was brutally fast in a killing dive, much faster than the others. But at the business of endlessly riding wisps of breeze I was weak.

I split off from Marco, circled to the right, and kept my laser-focus eyes on Tobias, careful to stay within thought-speak range.

<OK, this is it,> Tobias said. <See the big car park down there? Track left a block.>

I was catching my first decent breeze, so I soared upwards as I searched the ground below. Then I saw it.

17

<Left of the car park . . . that's a super-market, right?> I asked. I was puzzled. From the air, almost every building just looks like a big rectangle. <It looks like they had some kind of fire.>

<Yep. Now, look closer,> Tobias advised. <See the plastic sheet across the left side of the shop? Look how the breeze blows it in. See?>

<It looks like the entire left wall was knocked in or something,> Rachel said. She was a bald eagle, riding high above me and further west.

<Exactly,> Tobias said. <Now, see the car park on that side? See the marks?>

I did. There were several long gouges torn in the tarmac. Long, straight gouges, in perfect alignment, pointing right towards the wrecked wall of the shop. A couple of dozen workmen seemed to be on the ground, rushing around to erect a plywood wall to conceal the hole.

Suddenly, I realized. I guess Marco did, too.

<Oh, man,> Marco said. <Oh, man.>

<You'd never notice it from ground level,> Tobias said smugly. <But from the bird's-eye view, it's pretty obvious.>

<Something hit the ground. It was moving fast. It skidded across the supermarket car park, hit the wall, ploughed inside, and started a fire,> I said.

<Exactamundo,> Tobias said.

<It must have happened late at night,>

Cassie pointed out. <Otherwise there would have been cars in the car park.>

<You still haven't seen the best thing yet,> Tobias said. <Take a run, one at a time, over the site. Check out who's in charge of the clean-up crew.>

I flapped hard, turned, flapped harder, and shot over the smoke-scarred shop.

I only caught a glimpse of the man who was directing the work crew. I couldn't quite believe what I saw.

<Chapman?> I asked.

<Chapman,> Tobias confirmed. <He's been here all day.>

Chapman is the assistant principal at our school. He's also a high-ranking Controller — a very important part of the Yeerk invasion.

<Why is the assistant principal from our school suddenly working construction?> Cassie asked, adding, <As if I couldn't guess.>

<Whatever this is, it must be important,> Rachel said. <They're working fast. And look! That guy there with the long coat? Up on the roof? I just caught a flash of a machine gun under his coat.>

There were six or seven men and women on the roof of the shop. They were looking around with the kind of steely, paranoid gaze you see on the faces of the president's Secret Service guys.

<They're nervous,> Cassie agreed. <Scared,

19

even. You can see from the way they move. The way they act. Someone screwed something up big time, and everyone down there is very afraid.>

<So? What do we do, oh fearless leader?> Marco asked.

He was asking me. The others like to act as if I'm in charge. I don't think of myself that way, not really. But you know, whatever. If it makes them feel better to think I'm the leader, fine.

It's just that when people treat you like a leader, you start acting like a leader. And like I said, that means making decisions. Even when you're just guessing.

<Yeah, what's the plan?> Rachel asked.

Flash!

Right in my face!

Big, glittering eyes, the only things shining in the darkness.

A muzzle open just enough to show long, curved fangs.

The face of an extremely big cat. Mountain lion? Leopard?

In a second it would lunge, open its jaws wide and —

Flash!

<Whoa!> I yelled.

<What's the matter? Do you see something?> Tobias asked.

<Jake? I asked you, what's the plan?> Rachel said, sounding annoyed.

20

I was back in the air. I was flying. I was in falcon morph. Below me I saw the supermarket.

But I was totally confused. My mind wouldn't focus on reality. It was still in some jungle I'd never seen, staring into the eyes of a beautiful, deadly predator. What was happening to me? Was I going crazy?

<Um . . . um, I . . . I guess we'd better take a closer look, huh?> I managed to say.

<Definitely. Let's work up a plan. Let's do it,> Rachel said with her usual enthusiasm.

<Rachel, why is it whenever I hear you say "let's do it" my blood runs cold?> Marco asked.

<Let's see. Because you're a wimp?> Rachel speculated.

<Whatever this is, they're trying to clean it up fast. We have no time,> I said. <Better do this tonight.>

<Oh,> Rachel said. <Tonight? As in . . . *tonight?*> She didn't sound so enthusiastic any more.

<Oh, good,> Marco said sarcastically. <Another rushed, unplanned, last-minute mission. Those always turn out so well.>

Marco, I thought, *you don't know the half of it. Because in addition to all the other ways this could go bad, your "fearless leader" is losing his mind.*

Of course, I didn't say that. See, when you're the leader, you're not allowed to be crazy.

21

Chapter 4

<I hate this kind of stuff,> Marco said. <I hate rushing into things.>

We had landed in the woods. Landing, by the way, is the hardest part of flying. Taking off is scary, but landing is terrifying. See, the difference between landing and crashing is about four centimetres and four kilometres an hour.

We landed more or less gracefully on the pine needle floor of the forest. Tobias flew off to look for Ax. The rest of us demorphed.

<I seem to remember that the last time we rushed into something we managed to screw up the plan,> Cassie said. <On the other hand, we did survive.>

"Barely," Marco said, as he made the transition from mostly osprey to mostly human.

22

"It's just a supermarket," Rachel said with a shrug of shoulders that were just emerging. "Come on, how hard can it be?"

"How should we go in?" Marco wondered, looking at me.

I looked at Cassie. "Any suggestions?"

"We have a couple of morphs available for this job," she said. "Like Rachel said, it's a supermarket. A burnt-out supermarket, but a supermarket just the same. You'd expect there to be cockroaches, rats, flies . . ."

Suddenly, there came a rush of pounding hooves and a crash of underbrush. Ax raced up to us, graceful and bizarre all at once.

He ploughed straight towards us, moving as fast as a panicked horse. Just when I was sure he'd run us down, he kicked his hind legs and sailed easily over our heads.

He landed almost daintily, and turned back to face us.

Ax is Aximili-Esgarrouth-Isthill. He's the younger brother of Prince Elfangor. As far as we know, Ax is the only Andalite to survive the destruction of their Dome ship.

Andalites have certain things in common with Earth animals. But you'd know right off that he's from a long, long way away.

His body is like a sort of strong pale-blue-and-brown deer. But where the deer would have a neck, Ax has a somewhat human upper body.

It looks like the chest and shoulders of a boy. He has two weak-looking arms and a few too many fingers.

His head is where you'd expect to find it, but it is missing one very major ingredient: a mouth. Andalites eat by absorbing plants through their hollow hooves. And they communicate through thought-speak.

Ax has three small slits for a nose and two big, almond-shaped eyes. He also has two other eyes. These are mounted on top of his head on short stalks. These two eyes can move separately in any direction. It's distracting until you get used to it. Ax may look at you with his two main eyes, or he may look at you with both stalk eyes, or one stalk eye, or a combination of his two main eyes and one stalk eye.

To summarize: it's very strange making eye contact with an Andalite.

And last, but definitely not least, there's the tail. It's like a scorpion's tail, cocked up so that the deadly sharp blade on the end sort of hovers above Ax's shoulder.

The tail is fast. Very fast. As in, you're bleeding and wondering why you can only count to four on your fingers, before you even see it move. Fast, accurate, and very good to have on your side of a fight.

<Hello, everyone,> Ax said. <Tobias told me to hurry.>

Just then, Tobias swooped low overhead and landed with utter confidence on a branch. He dug his talons into the bark and began to calmly preen his wing feathers.

"Hi, Ax," I said. "What has Tobias told you?"

<Everything. I guess we are going in to take a closer look?>

"You guess right, Ax-man," Marco said. "You have a preference for fly or cockroach morph?"

<I will do whatever Prince Jake orders.>

"Ax, don't call me Prince Jake," I said automatically for about the thousandth time.

<Yes, Prince Jake,> he said.

Sometimes I wonder if maybe Ax has a sense of humour. We'd never noticed one, but who knows?

"We have to get inside that Safeway," I said. "The closest place to morph is a long way away. Clear across the street, behind that boarded-up motel. No one will see us there, but then we have to get to the shop. Across four lanes of traffic."

"Ouch," Marco said. "I hadn't really thought about that. Is it too late for me to change my vote?"

"We didn't vote," Rachel said. "But if we had, you'd have voted yes."

"How do you know how I'd have voted?" Marco demanded.

Rachel smiled. "Because I'd have voted yes.

25

And you'd never let yourself look like a total wimp in front of girls."

"You think you know me," Marco said. "Unfortunately, you're right."

"Neither the roach nor the fly has very good vision," Rachel pointed out. "I mean, we want to be able to see whatever is in that shop, right?"

"Yeah, but we also have to get across four lanes of traffic. I don't know about you, but I'd rather fly over the cars than try to walk in front of them," Cassie said.

"Can flies even find their way that far?" I wondered out loud.

"Remember when we used to have normal, sane conversations?" Marco said. "You know, we'd talk about baseball or who had a crush on who?"

Cassie gave him a wink. Then, she was back to business. "That supermarket must still be full of food, right? Rotting food, since I doubt the freezers are working in there. What's better at finding rotting food than a fly?"

<I can help guide you, maybe,> Tobias said.

"You don't see that much better than humans do in the dark," I pointed out. "It'll be dark by the time we get in position."

<Car lights . . . streetlights . . . I'm just saying maybe I can help a little, all right?>

Tobias sometimes becomes frustrated because he can't go on all the missions. I understand. I feel sorry for him. But that's the way it is. I was about to tell him that when Cassie jumped in.

"Tobias, the only reason we even *know* about this is you," Cassie pointed out. "You discovered it. You showed it to us. The least we can do is take the next step."

Cassie is so good at fixing hurt feelings. Better than me, that's for sure. But Tobias was still grumpy. <I'm still going along,> he said.

"OK," I said, clapping my hands together and trying to sound cheerful and optimistic. "Flies it is. Everyone go home. We meet behind the motel in. . ." I checked my watch, "in approximately three hours. Around seven forty-five or so. We do a quick morph, we're in and out of that Safeway in ten minutes and back home again."

"Oh, man," Marco groaned. "I hate it when you try to sound cheerful, Jake. It always means you're worried. Next you'll flash that big 'no-sweat' grin. I know you."

"Three hours to fly time," I said, forcing up a big, confident grin.

"We're dead meat," Marco said.

27

Chapter 5

5:15 P.M.

"Hi, Dad, what's up?" I asked when I got home. My father was in his lounger, remote control in hand.

"What do you mean, 'what's up'?" he asked, genuinely surprised. "The fight's on tonight. Forty dollars on Pay-Per-View. Corn crisps, bean dip, loud grunting male noises, beer — for me — soda for you and Tom."

I practically slapped my forehead. The fight! I'd totally forgotten. It was a big thing. Not because I'm a boxing fanatic. I'm not. But it was a big thing for my dad to actually spend forty dollars on pay-per-view. He was doing it as a male-bonding, father–son thing. Me and him and Tom, and probably one or two of my dad's friends from work.

"That's *tonight*?" I asked. "What time?"

"Starts at seven o'clock. Do your homework, eat something containing vegetables to make your mum happy, and then grab some sofa."

I did a quick mental calculation. The fight started in a little over an hour. The last championship fight had lasted only three rounds. That would leave me maybe thirty minutes to morph and fly to the motel.

Should I come up with some excuse for bailing out? No. No, there was no way my dad would buy it.

"Excellent," I said to my dad. "I'll be here. Don't eat all the bean dip. You know what happens when you eat bean dip."

My mother came into the living room. "Am I even allowed in here?" she asked mockingly. "When does this room become the temple of male aggression?"

"Not till seven," my dad said. "Until then we will allow females. Especially if the females remembered to pick up crisps on their way home from work."

"Crisps? Wouldn't you rather enjoy some nice carrot sticks and hummus dip?"

My dad and I just stared at her.

"Kidding," she said. "Just kidding. I have crisps. Are Pete and Dominick coming over?"

"Yeah, but you don't have to feed them," my dad joked. "Those guys are lucky I don't charge

29

them admission."

I raced through my homework and hoped the fight would be the usual two-or-three-round easy knockout. The one good thing about rushing was that it didn't leave me too much time to think. Thinking meant worry, and worry gets in the way of getting things done.

It was a tense family gathering at seven o'clock. Tom seemed as anxious as I was to get away. I could guess why.

You see, Tom is one of them. He's a human-Controller.

He had to keep up appearances of normality, same as me. But I guess he was trying to get away to go to the supermarket site, too. Same as me, again.

Tom and I fought in the same war. On different sides.

It was strange thinking of Tom, still alive deep down inside his own head. Trapped. Powerless. But able to see and hear and think.

Did he enjoy watching the fight through eyes he no longer controlled? Was there anything, anything at all, he could enjoy?

It didn't help, having thoughts like that. When I started thinking that way the rage would just build up inside me till I felt like I'd go nuclear. I told myself, for probably the millionth time, that I was doing all I could to help Tom. All I could.

All I could.

Fortunately, my dad and his work friends made plenty of noise, so no one noticed Tom checking his watch. Or the fact that I kept glancing towards the kitchen, where I could see the wall clock.

By round six, I knew I was in trouble. In round seven neither fighter even looked tired. I decided if it went past round eight I'd have to make some excuse, no matter how lame.

In round eight, a lucky uppercut connected.

"Oh, that had to hurt!" my dad said.

"Five bucks says he goes down!" my dad's friend Dominick said quickly.

He was right. The challenger staggered, wandered around on rubber legs for a few seconds, then toppled over. Boom! The fight was over.

It was now seven forty-five. I was already late.

I snatched the tape out of the video. "Dad, can I take this over to Marco's and play it for him?"

"It's almost eight. It's dark out," my father objected.

"Yeah," Tom said. "You might get lost and never come back. And that would be such a pity. I'd have to use your room for my weights and stuff."

It was exactly the kind of dumb big-brother joke Tom would have made. But of course it was just something pulled up from Tom's brain by the Yeerk in his head.

For just a second it occurred to me to ask him: "Hey, Tom, what's the big secret with the supermarket? Just tell me, and I can stay at home tonight."

I smiled at the thought. Then. . .

FLASH!

Green. Green. Everything was green. It was the greenest place on Earth: trees, moss, vines, ferns. Green everywhere.

Marco was there. And the others. They were all there.

Marco was talking. ". . .in a jungle fighting brain-stealing aliens and ten thousand annoying species of bugs, and our resident space cadet is a hot-looking monkey. Somebody wake me up when we get back to reality."

FLASH!

I was back. Back listening to Tom tease me as if he was actually Tom. Back to hearing my dad say, "Walk, don't ride your bike. Not at night. Especially not when it's about to rain."

The vision was so powerful. So real. Not like a dream at all. But like I was actually there in a jungle, listening to Marco complain.

I felt my heart pounding. I felt sweat forming on my forehead.

What in the heck was going on? What was happening to me?

I noticed Tom back out of the room, sliding away like he was going to the kitchen. That brought me back to reality.

I grabbed the tape and took off, still reeling from the insane feeling of being yanked back and forth from one reality to another.

I could hear my dad and his friends rehashing the fight round by round as I went up to my room and opened my window as wide as it would go.

It took me twenty-five minutes to morph and fly to the empty motel.

<I know, I know, I'm late,> I apologized as I came in for a landing.

I misjudged the distance to the ground, hit it too hard, and rolled over, a tangle of wings and talons.

<Nice landing,> Tobias said with a laugh.

"Are you OK?" Cassie asked me. She rushed over and picked me up. Then she set me back down because I was starting to demorph. And I was getting heavier pretty quickly.

"I'm fine," I said, as soon as I could speak. "Embarrassed, but fine."

It was a shabby little hiding place. The back windows of the motel were covered in plywood. The plywood was covered with graffiti. There were overgrown weeds and broken bottles and, for some reason, an old washing machine.

"We get to visit all the best places, don't

33

we?" I said drily.

Ax was hugging the darkness against the wall. He feels a little obvious out of the woods. With good reason. Anyone who saw him would run away, screaming like a little kid. Unless, of course, they were a Controller. A Controller would know exactly what he was.

"Well?" Rachel asked, looking at me.

She was waiting for me to say, "Let's go."

But for some reason, I felt a strange reluctance. I felt . . . I don't even know what I felt. Just that that moment, that very moment, was terribly important.

The others all stared at me, waiting.

All I had to say was, "Let's go." Instead, I looked at my watch. Eight-nineteen. Eight-nineteen. Like it meant something. Like. . .

Oh, man, I was going nuts! I was losing it. What was the matter with me?

"Should we do this?" I wondered. I was surprised to realize I'd spoken out loud. I'd been talking to myself.

"Why not? I say we do it," Rachel said.

"There's a huge shock," Marco muttered. "Everyone who is surprised Rachel wants to go for it, raise your hand."

"Yeah," I said, shaking off my doubts as well as I could. "Yeah, let's go."

I was pretty sure it was the right thing to do, but the responsibility was on me. I could have

34

stopped it. I could have talked them all out of it. I could have done something different.

But I didn't.

At least not then. . .

"Let's morph," I said.

Chapter 6

"Let's hope no one has a can of Raid," Marco said.

I tried to laugh. But I hate morphing bugs.

Back when we started morphing, I figured we'd morph things like lions and bears and eagles. And we do. But we also morph things a lot smaller. The insect world is very useful. Sometimes smaller is better.

That never exactly makes it fun, though. There is no nightmare, no horror movie, no weird psycho vision as scary as actually turning into a cockroach or a spider or a flea or a fly.

When you morph a tiger, you still have four limbs. You have two eyes. You have a mouth. You have bones and a stomach and lungs and teeth. Maybe they're all different, but they're all

36

still there.

The change to a fly is nothing like becoming a tiger. Nothing is where it should be. Nothing stays the same.

The problem with morphs is that they are never exactly the same twice in a row. And the changes happen in bizarre, unpredictable ways. It's not smooth. It's not logical. It's not gradual.

I started to shrink, but when I was still almost entirely human, still probably a metre tall, I felt my skin harden.

See, flies don't have bones. They have an exoskeleton. Their outer shell is what holds them together in one piece. And my exoskeleton was growing. My soft, human skin was being replaced by something dark, something hard as plastic.

My body was squeezed into segments. Insect segments: a head, a thorax, an abdomen.

And when I was still at least half a metre tall, way too tall to be anything like a fly, the extra legs came bursting, squishing, slurping out of what had been my chest.

My own true legs collapsed as they shrivelled down to match my new fly legs. I fell forwards into the dirt. Face down. Not that I had much of a face any more.

My proboscis had already begun to form from my melting mouth and lips and nose and tongue. The proboscis was as big as my fly legs — a long, retractable, hollow tube. Flies eat with the proboscis. They spit saliva all over the food, wait till it gets mushy, then suck it up.

It isn't pretty.

But that wasn't the worst of it. The worst was the eyes. I still had semi-human vision when I saw Cassie, lying in the dirt beside me, suddenly grow fly eyes.

They popped out of her human eyes. Popped out, huge and devoid of soul. Big, black balloons that sort of inflated out of her own eye sockets.

That's a sight that will make you heave up your lunch.

My own vision went dark then. I was blind for a couple of seconds, then yow! The fly eyes turned on, and the whole world was different.

How can I explain what it's like to look through compound eyes? It's like you're watching a thousand tiny TV sets all at once. A thousand tiny TV sets, all clustered together. And each set has really weird colour. Like someone twisted all the colour knobs. Yellow is purple, green is red, blue is black. It's insane. Like some disturbed kid got loose with a Crayola box and coloured in everything with different colours.

But what's awful is the way the eyes look in all directions at once. I could see the tube, that was now my mouth, sticking out in front of me. I could see my own twig legs. I could see the stiff hairs poking out of my armoured body.

Still, there is one good thing about being a fly — if you can get past the screaming horror of it. Part of what I could see was the pair of gossamer wings that sprouted from what should have been my back.

Flies can fly.

Man, can they fly.

<Everyone OK?> I asked.

<Aside from the fact I make myself sick? Yes,> Marco said.

Then . . . PAH-LOOOSH!

An explosion on the ground ahead of me. The dirt just seemed to blow up. Like a mortar explosion.

<What the . . .> Rachel yelped.

PAH-LOOOSH!

<It's starting to rain, guys,> Tobias informed us calmly.

The explosions of mortar shells were just big, fat raindrops hitting the dirt.

<Jeez! I thought someone was trying to kill us,> Cassie said.

<Let's get on with this,> I said.

I fired the springs in my legs and turned on my wings. I was airborne instantly. It's not like being a bird. A bird has to really work at flying. For a fly, it's automatic. Instantaneous. You think *let's fly* and a split second later you're zooming crazily through the air.

Across the weird mass of tiny TV sets I could see the others rise up from the ground. They flew like pigs. Like big fat balls with these tiny little wings that looked like they couldn't lift a speck of dust.

But, like I said before, flies *can* fly.

I zoomed wildly upwards. Like a wallowing rocket!

<Hah-HAH! Oh, man!> Rachel exulted. <I'd forgotten how great this was!>

<Disgusting, but oh yeah, these things can move,> Marco agreed. <Tobias, you only think you can fly. You haven't flown till you've flown Maggot Airways.>

<Maybe so,> Tobias said calmly. <And, not to burst your balloon, but you guys are all heading the wrong way.>

<We are?>

<Yes. You're heading towards a dump-bin,> Tobias said with a laugh. <Turn left. Turn left and get some altitude. Then you should be able to see the car lights on the road.>

I would have smiled if I'd had a mouth. The fly brain had been easy to control because we'd already done this morph before. But the fly's instincts still had some input. See, the fly smelled rotting food in the dump-bin and it knew right where it wanted to go.

We followed Tobias's directions. I rocketed higher, and then. . .

<Whoa! Whoa! What is that? Are those cars?> Cassie demanded.

<These eyes are seeing ultra-violet light,> Ax commented.

<They're seeing something, that's for sure,> I agreed.

The cars racing past were not cars so much as they were glowing, red-and-purple meteors. The road was a blur of movement, all of it strange and disturbing to the fly brain.

<Stay above the cars,> Tobias warned.

<Why?> Ax asked.

<A little something we call windscreens,> Tobias said drily. <A windscreen moving a hundred kilometres an hour is death to bugs.>

<Good point,> I agreed. <Going higher.>

I powered my wings and bobbed and weaved and rolled higher and higher.

But the fly inside my head didn't like it. He lived close to the ground. The ground was where you found food. And food was all the fly brain cared about.

<It's starting to rain harder,> Tobias said.

I began to notice more drops. They were sparkling meteorites, each three times my own size. They plummeted around me. But in my fly scale of things they were fairly far apart.

Then . . . more rain.

Closer together. Falling thick and fast all around me.

41

WHAM!

<Ahhhh!>

I was slammed.

I tumbled through the air, covered in something like heavy glue.

Water! Just water, but sticky as glue to my fly body.

My wings shook off the water and I found myself flying upside down. I spun around and advanced again.

<Oh, man,> I complained. <This is a whole new reason not to like rain!>

<I'm going ahead,> Tobias said tensely. <Raining too hard. I've got to land.>

WHAM!

A glancing blow from a raindrop the size of a truck. It spun me around in the air.

<Ahhhhhhh! Man!>

<Jake! Are you OK?!> Cassie cried.

Once again, those amazing fly wings turned me around and kept me in the air. But suddenly I realized I was in a sea of brilliant lights.

Purple! Red! Green!

Green?

Motion! Every hair on my nasty fly body felt it. Every screen in my fly eyes sensed it.

Something moving. Fast! Big!

A monstrous wall came at me with impossible speed! It was a mountain! Huge. Tall. Sloped. A mountain moving a hundred kilometres an hour right at me, glowing in a rainbow of eerie colours!

A windscreen!

<Uh-oh,> I said.

Chapter 7

<YAAAAAHHHH!> I screamed in thought-speak as the deadly windscreen blew towards me.

Flash!

The jungle! Sudden movement in the deep bush.

A cocked arm.

A *human* arm belonging to a kid!

A spear flew!

I saw it coming for me. Saw the bamboo point, blackened with deadly poison.

One scratch and I was dead.

I —

Flash!

Spear! No, *windscreen!*

My wings beat the air at hundreds of strokes per second. I was fast, but not fast enough.

44

A down draught! A vicious wind that sucked me towards the windscreen. I fought it, then . . . in a split second, the wind became a magic carpet.

The power of my wings, the slipstream of wind . . . I missed the top of the windscreen by a millimetre!

I could actually see colour-distorted human faces inside the car.

I saw their glowing eyes as I flew past and over and seriously hauled my little fly butt up and up and up.

<Jake? You still with us, Jake?> Rachel asked.

<Oh, yeah,> I said. <Barely. But I'm here. You know, they really need to lower the speed limit. Cars shouldn't go more than maybe fifteen kilometres per hour.>

We passed the road and left the eerie stream of fast lights behind us. We all got slammed by more raindrops, but personally, I was past caring about that.

Then, even through the cleansing rain, I began to smell the supermarket.

The fly sensed food.

We didn't need Tobias to guide us the rest of the way. Our fly bodies were eager to head for the smell of rotting rubbish.

I was still reeling from the twin sensations of being attacked by a windscreen and a spear.

The jungle visions were so real. They were so absolutely real. I mean, I felt every single thing while I was in them. I felt heat and humidity on my skin, I felt bugs buzzing my face, I felt. . .

But I didn't have time for that now.

The Safeway was beyond our ability to see. I mean, it was just so big it had no meaning to our fly eyes. What had meaning to the fly was that there was food up ahead.

We zipped in under the plastic sheeting that covered the damaged wall. Once inside the shop, everything was very bright. I saw brilliant lights that seemed to be spewing a whole rainbow of unusual colours.

There were people walking around below us. There was machinery moving. And there was a mound, a mountain of food all shovelled into one corner.

The Controllers had simply used earth-movers to shove all the shelves, the freezers, the refrigerators, the loose cans, the glass meat display case, the doughnuts and cupcakes from the bakery area, the flowers, the cooked chicken and beans . . . everything that had been in the shop, all into one corner.

<You know,> Marco said, <if you threw in some dog poop, this would be fly heaven.>

<We are not alone,> Ax pointed out. <There seem to be many others of this species here.>

He was right. We had chosen the right

morph. There had to be ten thousand flies in that shop. I could hear them and smell them and even see them as they flew past.

<Well, no one is going to notice us, that's for sure,> Cassie said. <We could dive right in.>

<Excuse me? Hello? We're not here to eat rubbish and make maggots,> I said. <We are in and out, so let's pay attention. What's going on here?>

<Well . . . there's that big thing in the middle of the room,> Cassie said. <That's what all the Controllers are clustered around.>

<Let's get closer,> I suggested.

We zipped in our crazy fly way towards the middle of the shop. There was a huge object there. As big as a small house, I would have guessed. But it's hard to tell how big something is when you're less than a centimetre long.

<Wait . . . I think I hear Chapman's voice,> Cassie said.

<I don't know how you can make sense out of all this noise,> Rachel grumbled.

<I've done the fly morph more than you have,> Cassie said. <Remember, I was in fly morph when I spied on Chapman at the shopping mall. There he is! I'm going closer.>

I couldn't see where Cassie was going or where she landed. One fly looks pretty much like the next. And the shop was like a fly airport. Flies were zipping all around.

<Cassie? Where are you?>

<I'm close to Chapman,> she said. <On his head, actually. On the bald spot.>

<Get off there! He could swat you!>

<Wait . . . I'm listening. . .>

I buzzed around aimlessly, afraid for Cassie, and trying to figure out what on Earth the big . . . *thing* . . . was.

<Whoa!> Cassie said. <Whoa! Whoa!>

<What? What? What?> I asked.

<Whoa!>

<What whoa?!> I practically yelled in frustration. <What's going on?!>

<It's a Bug fighter,> Cassie said. <It's something new. An experimental Bug fighter. Faster, more weapons . . . a new, prototype Bug fighter.>

Bug fighters are the small, basic Yeerk spacecraft. They look like a streamlined cockroach with two long, serrated spears pointing forward. Those are the Dracon beams.

<What's it doing *here*? In a Safeway?> Marco asked.

<It crashed. Duh,> Rachel said.

<I don't know,> Cassie said. <Chapman isn't talking about how it got here. He's just telling this other Controller it has to be out of here in three hours or Visser Three is going to be madder than he already is. The guy says it's almost ready to go, he just needs to run some

tests. Three hours will be no problem. Chapman says, "Good, because if it's three hours and one minute, I'll personally feed you to Visser Three for a snack.">

<Three hours?> Tobias said.

I was surprised to hear his thought-speak voice. <Tobias! I thought you went for cover.>

<The rain stopped,> he said. <And I can see down into the shop. They've knocked a hole in the roof so the security guys up on the roof can get down into the shop quickly. There's a ladder. I'm flying over.>

<What do you see up there?>

<A bunch of nervous human-Controllers with machine guns.>

<What should we do?> Rachel wondered. <In three hours they could fly this thing out of here.>

<If only we could get some TV news-people here,> Cassie mused. <If people could see this thing, and have proof. . .>

<The Yeerks have too many people at the local TV stations and newspapers,> I pointed out.

<You know what we *could* do, though?> Rachel began.

<Uh-oh, a suggestion from Rachel,> Marco groaned.

<What we could do is steal this thing.>

<Steal it and do what with it?> Tobias wondered.

49

I laughed. <We could always steal it and fly it to Washington and land it on the White House lawn. Let the Yeerks try and cover *that* up.>

I meant it as a joke.

Really. A joke.

<Hey,> Rachel said. <That could work.>

<Ax? Can you fly that thing?> Tobias asked.

<I am an Andalite,> Ax said. <That's just a Yeerk fighter, even if it is experimental. No second-rate Yeerk technology is too sophisticated for me.>

<But . . . we'd have to do this like right now,> Cassie pointed out.

<Yep,> Rachel said. <Right now. Jake?>

<There can't be many people *inside* the Bug fighter,> Ax pointed out. <They usually only have a crew of two. At most there would be four or five technicians inside, Prince Jake.>

<Yeah, well, four or five people versus five houseflies is not good odds for us,> I said. It was moments like this that I resented. Moments when I tended to make the decisions. And when I would carry the responsibility. <Still. . .>

<I hear the gears in Jake's little brain grinding away,> Marco joked.

<Still,> I said. <There may be a way.>

Chapter 8

8:32 P.M.

<**O**K, fellow flies, into the Bug fighter.>

We zoomed crazily around the outside of the huge-seeming Bug fighter till we spotted a door. Inside we saw the blurry, strangely coloured shapes of humans. Actually, human-Controllers.

We buzzed right on inside.

<I count five people,> Rachel said.

<Just what we expected,> I said. I was trying to sound confident, to help everyone else stay calm. But I was tense. I was on edge. This was a spur-of-the-moment plan thought up by a guy who was having jungle hallucinations. It was a desperate, possibly stupid plan. I didn't know for sure. It could easily end with Tobias dead. Maybe the rest of us as well.

51

But Tobias was thrilled to be playing a major role.

<Tobias? You ready?>

<Any time you say, Jake.>

<Once around the room, that's it,> I warned him.

<You're the boss,> Tobias said.

<OK. Now!>

Outside, above the supermarket, Tobias had been gaining altitude. Which was extremely difficult in the cool night air. Hawks are not night birds. But Tobias flapped his way up and up, always keeping sight of the bright hole in the supermarket's roof.

<Here I come!> Tobias yelled.

He plunged at maximum speed, straight for the hole in the roof. <I'm inside!>

I could tell, because right away there was shouting. Yelling. Orders being barked out.

Then. . .

BLAM! BLAM! BLAM!

Gunfire! They were shooting at him!

<These guys couldn't hit . . . yikes! That was close!>

The plan called for Tobias to provide a distraction. The Yeerks knew we used bird morphs. And they would know that a hawk did not belong flying around inside a shop. They would put two and two together. They would know Tobias was not a real hawk.

BLAM! BLAM! BLAMBLAMBLAMBLAM!

Someone was firing a machine gun. Even with my vague fly hearing I could hear the air shaking with the noise. Hundreds of rounds were being fired inside that shop!

A human voice yelled something like, "Get out here and help! It's an Andalite bandit in morph!"

That's what the Yeerks think we are: Andalites.

The technicians inside the Bug fighter went piling out of the exit, glad of the chance to take shots at an Andalite "bandit".

<That's enough, Tobias! Bail out! Bail out of here!> I yelled. <Ax! Morph! Everyone morph! Now! Now! Now!>

BLAMBLAMBLAMBLAMBLAM!

<Can't get out!> Tobias cried. <The guys on the roof are shooting down through the hole!>

Of course! Why hadn't I realized that? Of course they would block Tobias's escape.

I was still mostly fly, but morphing as fast as I could. I could feel myself getting bigger. I could see my fly wings shrivelling away.

Tobias couldn't escape. They'd get him. Sooner or later, no matter how fast he flew, they'd get him. An answer . . . an answer . . . I needed an answer. I needed to—

<Tobias! Tobias! This way,> I yelled. <Inside the Bug fighter!>

<No, that will draw them after — YAH! Whoa! That one clipped my tail feathers!>

<Come inside!> I yelled.

<Whatever you say,> Tobias said.

My human eyes were just re-emerging as Tobias blew in through the door of the Bug fighter. I looked left. A horrifying creature with a small scorpion tail and fly legs and a semi-humanoid face with a gigantic proboscis was trying to work the controls of the ship with clumsy fly stick legs. It was Ax, halfway through morphing.

Suddenly, the door shut. Or in this case, the bulkhead simply dimpled and closed up again, eliminating the door.

"They're in the Bug fighter!" I heard Chapman howl in rage. "They're in the Bug fighter! Get them!"

I was mostly human now, but still at that stage where I wouldn't have wanted to see myself in a mirror. The rest were coming out of morph, too. Cassie was fastest, as usual. She was already checking Tobias for wounds.

Ax was almost fully Andalite once more.

"Ax, get us outta here!" I said, as my human mouth returned.

<Yes, Prince Jake.>

I didn't waste time telling him not to call me "Prince".

<These are unusual controls,> Ax admitted. BAP!BAP!BAP!BAP!BAP!

Bullets rattled against the Bug fighter's outer skin.

Then I heard the grinding sounds of the engine. Through the cockpit window, I saw the Controllers turning big earth-movers towards us.

"They're going to ram us!" Marco warned.

"Ax?" I asked tersely.

<I think I . . . I don't know. Prince Jake, I can try but it may not work.>

"Just do it!" I yelled.

There was a whirring noise. Lights came on all over the cockpit. A sound like a low siren.

<I found the "on" switch,> Ax said.

"Great," Marco said. "Now find the get-us-the-heck-outta-here switch!"

I felt the ship lift up off the Safeway floor. It rose just a metre and sort of wallowed slightly, side to side. The heavy equipment was still coming for us.

Ax turned the fighter, pointing it towards the missing wall.

<Is that plastic sheeting very strong?> Ax asked.

"Let's find out," I said.

Then . . . WHOOOOOOOSH!

It was like getting kicked in the chest. We all tumbled backwards — all but Ax, who has four legs. The acceleration was incredible. The Bug fighter rocketed forwards. We blew through the plastic sheeting.

We blew across the car park.

We arched up towards the dark night sky.

"We did it!" Rachel yelled.

<Sorry about the acceleration,> Ax said. <I forget that humans fall over easily.>

"Just get us out of here, Ax," Marco said. "We're going to Washington, DC, to meet the President."

Chapter 9

It was crowded inside the Bug fighter. Especially because Ax takes up a lot of room.

But we huddled together and looked over Ax's shoulders as he worked the controls. And we looked past Ax, out through the transparent panels at the front of the Bug fighter.

<This ship is very difficult to handle,> Ax said. <The design is strange. Some controls are psychotronic. But others require physical handling. Unfortunately, those controls are designed for Taxxons. They have more hands than I.>

"Can we do anything to help?" I asked.

<Someone should take weapons station,> Ax said.

"Cool," Marco said. He leaped forward, but I

57

was closer.

I slipped into the area beside Ax. Ax's pilot "seat" wasn't a seat at all, of course. Taxxons are like huge centipedes, so they can't really sit. Which was good, because Ax doesn't sit, either.

But the weapons station was built for Hork-Bajir. Hork-Bajir are two metres tall and have thick, spiky tails, but they do sit.

"No *way* you should handle the weapons," Marco said, leaning over my shoulder. "I kick your butt in video games."

"Yeah, right," I said. "In some alternative universe, maybe."

"Grab the joystick," Marco suggested.

As strange as it seems, there actually was a joystick. It was for much bigger hands than mine, and the two buttons on it were clumsy to reach. But it was a joystick.

"Maybe I should test the weapons," I said to Ax.

<Yes,> he said tersely, distracted.

We were rising up through the atmosphere. We were above the clouds already. I could see brief flashes of the lights of the city down below, but mostly it was clouds and more clouds.

But we weren't rising as fast as I would have expected. Ax was definitely working to control the ship.

I looked ahead, saw nothing in the way, and pressed one of the buttons on the joystick.

Nothing.

Ax glanced over. <That was the safety. The Dracon beam should be armed now. See the screen before you? The red circle is how you aim. Use a combination of moving the joystick, but also use your mind.>

Marco put his hand on my shoulder. "Phasers on full power!" he said in a Captain Picard English accent. "Arm photon torpedoes! If the Borg want a fight, we'll give them one! Make it so!"

I moved the joystick and watched the target circle track across the screen. It still showed nothing but starry sky. That should be safe enough.

I squeezed the second button.

TSEWWWW! TSEWWWW!

Twin red beams of light fired forwards, converging too far away for me to see.

"Yes! Most splendid!" Marco yelled.

"OK, that *was* cool," I admitted, trying not to cackle like an idiot with his first video game.

"Boys with their toys," Cassie teased gently.

<Prince Jake?> Ax said. <I must apologize.>

"Why?"

<I did not at first realize: this Bug fighter's cloaking field is not working.>

It took a few seconds for me to track on that. "You mean . . . people can see us?"

<The clouds will hide us from people on the

59

ground,> Ax said. <But human radar will observe us. In fact, they have already observed us.>

"Uh-oh. Maybe we better get higher," I suggested.

<Yes. But we are rising slowly. I don't know why. And there are two objects approaching us.>

"Probably just airliners," Rachel said.

<The objects are moving at one and a half times the speed of sound,> Ax said.

"OK, that's not a passenger plane," Marco said.

I groaned. "Military jets. Oh, man, it's the Air Force after us. They're 'good guys.' They're on our side. We can't shoot them down."

Suddenly. . .

SWOOOOOSH!

SWOOOOOSH!

Two pale grey jets blew past us. The backwash rattled the Bug fighter.

<I can access their radio signals,> Ax said. And a second later we heard the voice of one of the pilots.

"Um . . . Base Control, I . . . um . . . Bogie is of an unknown type. Say again, unknown type."

"Definitely unknown," the other pilot said. "Way unknown."

"We're coming around for another pass."

I looked at Ax. "We really don't want to get shot down by a couple of F-sixteens."

<No, Prince Jake. That would be embarrassing. I believe I now know how to increase—>

FAH-WHOOOOOOOM!

Suddenly, we were out of there. Out of the clouds. Out of the atmosphere.

"Yes! This thing can move!" Marco exulted. "We need to buy this game."

We heard a fainter, crackling voice over the radio. "Did you see that? Did you see that thing move, Colonel? Did you see that? What the—"

Then we were out of range, still zooming straight up into black space. Below us I could see the curvature of the Earth. It looked just like one of those pictures the shuttle astronauts take from up in orbit.

"That's so beautiful," Cassie said. "Look at that! You can see daylight coming up over the Red Sea."

<Excuse me,> Tobias said, <but I don't think the Red Sea is exactly on the way to Washington, DC.>

"Yeah, I guess not," I said. Although it was such a wonderful sight that I almost didn't want to worry about where we were going. "Ax, maybe we'd better slow down, get some idea of where Washington is and—"

<No! No!> Ax snapped.

I was shocked. Ax is always polite.

<No, Prince Jake,> he said, a little more calmly. <We cannot slow down.>

61

"What's the matter?" Cassie asked him.

Ax pointed at one of the view screens before him. On the screen I saw stars. Then the moon came into view, a vast grey-and-white light bulb.

And silhouetted against the glowing moon was a shape. It was like some medieval battle-axe. The rear half was a two-headed blade. From the middle, like an axe handle, extended a long shaft. At the end of the shaft was a triangular head, very much like an arrow's point.

It was black on black. And even if you had never seen it before and had no idea what it was, you'd know right away it was death.

I *had* seen it. I *knew* what it was.

"The Blade ship," I whispered.

The Blade ship of Visser Three.

Chapter 10

Visser Three, leader of the Yeerk invasion of Earth.

Visser Three, the only Yeerk in all of history to take control of an Andalite body.

Visser Three, the only Yeerk with the power to morph.

"Can we outrun him?" I asked Ax.

<No.>

"Can we outfight him?" I asked. My voice was a whisper. My mouth was too dry to work right.

Ax turned his stalk eyes to look at me. <No, Prince Jake. We might get in a lucky shot. But the Blade ship is very powerful. This is the Blade ship that destroyed our great Dome ship.>

"Here he comes!" Rachel yelled in warning.

63

A red glow illuminated the Blade ship as the Visser fired his engines and came for us.

<We can try and run. Or we can take a chance on a lucky shot,> Ax said.

He was looking at me. They were all looking at me. I grabbed the joystick. My hand was trembling.

"I feel lucky," I said. It was an absolute lie, of course. I didn't even feel *slightly* lucky. But it sounded good.

I caught Marco giving me a sardonic smile. He knew I was faking it.

I felt Cassie's hand touch my shoulder for encouragement.

<Hold on. You may be unsteady on your human legs,> Ax warned.

He threw the Bug fighter into a quick, tight turn. Ax was right. I almost fell over before the Bug fighter's systems compensated for inertia.

Then Ax really lit up the engines and we leaped forward, straight for the Blade ship.

<Ready to fire!> Ax said. It wasn't a question. <Not yet. Not yet. Not yet. Not yet. Wait until . . . NOW!>

I swept the red target circle towards the black-diamond head of the Blade ship. I squeezed the trigger. And I kept squeezing.

Brilliant Dracon beams stabbed towards the Blade ship.

But at the same instant, the Visser fired!

Dracon beam hit Dracon beam.

ZZZZZOOOOOWWWW!

An explosion of light so intense I could actually see *through* my own hand. I could see Cassie's teeth inside her head!

WHAAAMMMPPPH!

I was thrown against the ceiling.

I fell to the floor and rolled, out of control.

Rachel landed on top of me, knocking the wind out of me.

The Bug fighter was spinning. My eyes were filled with balls of light, like suns inside my own head.

Spinning . . . spinning . . . spinning. . .

And with each turn I was thrown hard. Into Ax. Into Marco. Tobias batted his wings wildly, trying to get some control. It was like we had all been tossed into a washer on spin cycle.

Then, with a sickening lurch, the Bug fighter came upright. There was a floor again. And a ceiling.

And through the window, there was a planet. Earth.

Big, blue, and getting closer very, very fast.

"We're going down!" Rachel yelled. "Ax! Ax! We're going down!"

Ax scrambled to his hooves and made his way back to the controls. <Too fast!> he said. <We're going down too fast!>

<Look!> Tobias cried. <Over there. To the

65

left. We're not alone.>

Tumbling down alongside us, just a kilo-metre away, was the Blade ship. It was twisting and twirling and falling, just like us.

"Wait. . ." Cassie said, sounding more con-fused than terrified. "It's daylight in the western hemisphere."

"Do I *care*?!" Marco yelled. "We're going down!"

"It was dawn in the Middle East," Cassie insisted. "Now it's daylight in the western hemisphere."

Suddenly, friction flames began glowing from the nose of the Bug fighter. We were going back into the atmosphere.

"Ax, can you pull us out of this?" I demanded.

<I am slowing our descent,> he said. <We are slowing down. But . . . but I don't think it will be enough.>

"Great," Marco moaned.

"At least the Blade ship will go down with us," Rachel said.

"Does that make you feel better, Xena?" Marco grated.

Rachel actually smiled. It was a sad, brief smile. "Not much better," she admitted.

<Ten seconds to impact!> Ax said. <Ten . . . nine . . . eight. . .>

Flash!

I was no longer in the Bug fighter.

I was square dancing.

I was giving Rachel a resentful look as I bowed to her in time with the music.

What the. . .

Flash!

<Four . . . three . . . hold on!>

I saw green. Green on green, rushing up at me.

And then we hit.

And for a while, I didn't see anything at all.

Chapter 11

Time Unknown

HOO! HOO! HOO! HOO! HOOHOHOHOHOHO! HAH! HAH!

KEEYAAAH! KEEYAAAH! KEEYAAAH!

I woke up.

I woke up very suddenly.

KEEYAAAH! KEEYAAAH! KEEYAAAH! YAHAHAHAHAH!

My head hurt, and the screaming noises didn't help. My back hurt, too.

I was lying on the ground. On mildewed, rotting leaves. Trees towered over me. Insanely tall trees. Ferns dipped down to tickle my face. There was a root or something under my back, which explained the back pain.

But I was alive.

KeRAW! KeRAW! KeRAW!

VrrEEET! VrrEEEET! VrrEEEET!

I sat up quickly. But that sent a spear of pain through my head. "Oh, man," I groaned.

Then I saw the bug. The bug on my lap. The big, giant, MONSTER bug. I guess it was some kind of beetle. It had yellow and black stripes and something that looked almost like curved antlers. I swear it was fifteen centimetres long. Or at least seven centimetres. It would have been beautiful, if it hadn't been *on me*.

"AAAAAHHH!" I yelled and brushed the beetle away.

Then, I felt the itchy, crawling feeling on my leg. Ants! There were a dozen ants climbing up my right shin.

I have been an ant. So you'd think maybe I have some sympathy for them. Wrong. I slapped at my leg till I was sure they were gone.

I climbed to my feet. I felt woozy and confused. Where was I? Where were the others?

I looked around. Green. Green everywhere. I mean, *every*where.

"The visions," I said to no one.

I was in a jungle. I knew that for sure. I'd never been in a jungle before, but there was no doubt in my mind. Maybe it was the monkeys and birds screeching at an insane volume all around me in the trees that gave it away. Maybe it was the creepers and vines. Maybe it was a flash of an amazing red-and-blue bird flitting through the branches. Maybe it was the fact that beetles really shouldn't be as big as that beetle had been.

It was jungle, all right.

Just like it had been in the weird flashes I'd been experiencing since that afternoon while square dancing.

"That's what did it," I muttered. "It was the square dancing that drove me crazy." I decided to yell for the others. "Hey! Hey! Cassie! Marco!"

It was like my voice had no power. The sound was just swallowed by the trees and ferns and bushes.

"OK, get a grip, Jake. Try to remember. You were coming down in the Bug fighter. Obviously you crashed. Duh. So look for the Bug fighter. It can't be far away."

I glanced around me at the solid wall of green in every direction. The air was steaming with humidity. And the smells of overly sweet flowers and tropical rot made me feel like I was walking past some department store perfume counter.

Then I spotted a tree where the top half had been snapped off. I started walking, trying to get a better angle on the broken tree. I saw a second tree, splintered. I began to notice what looked like a tunnel ploughed through the dense foliage.

A tunnel ploughed through the trees and foliage should lead to the Bug fighter.

"Or the Blade ship," I reminded myself.

HOO! HOO! HOO! HOOHOOHOOHOO! HAH! HAH! HAH!

The jungle was quietening down a little, but there was still some fairly crazy screeching from up in the tall trees. The jungle animals sounded annoyed. Probably they didn't appreciate someone crashing a Bug fighter into their home. And they didn't like my looks, either.

The jungle floor was surprisingly clear. Down at foot level there wasn't much growing, just dead leaves. But at face level there were vines and bushes and ferns, all slapping me in the face as I pressed on.

Suddenly I came to a clearing. A hole in the canopy where a tree had fallen. Bright sunlight shone down through the gap. And it was as if every species of plant life you could imagine was crowding into that sunny spot. I found myself facing an incredible wall of vegetation: a dozen types of brilliant flowers, mosses so green they didn't seem real, small vines wrapped around bigger vines wrapped around tree trunks.

It was the greenest place on Earth. There were even plants growing out of the smooth trunks of tall trees.

I trudged on, back into the shadows of the forest, and when I looked up, I could no longer see the tunnel through the foliage.

That's when I started to get really scared.

I was in a jungle. And jungle isn't like forest, where you can usually see for hundreds of metres in any direction. Jungle presses in close around. It's like being buried in green.

Ger-AK! Ger-AK! AKAKAKAK!

"Marco! Cassie! Rachel!" I yelled, feeling the edge of panic.

<How about Tobias?> a voice said in my head.

I looked up and saw nothing. Then I noticed him swooping down towards me from the high branches of a tree.

"Tobias!" I yelled. I waved. Of course, he'd already seen me, obviously. But I was massively relieved. So I waved again.

The red-tailed hawk body seemed almost bland, boring in the context of this jungle. He landed on a rotting, moss-encrusted log.

"Tobias! The others?"

<Everyone is alive,> he said. <It took a while to find everyone, though. I think the Bug fighter must have spun around a few times tearing through the trees. Cassie ended up practically on top of this snake. This extremely large snake.>

"Where are we?"

<I don't know,> Tobias said. <But I'm pretty sure this ain't home. Come on, follow me. It's not far.>

I followed Tobias, pushing and shoving and fighting my way through forest that seemed determined to stop me. I was dripping with sweat and gasping in the thick air.

Then, a clearing. Not a natural clearing, but one created by the crashed Bug fighter.

"Jake!" Cassie yelled and ran over to give me a hug. She had a nasty cut on one hand, which she'd bandaged with strips torn from her T-shirt.

"You're alive," Marco observed. "For now," he added darkly.

"I told you he'd be OK," Rachel said.

The Bug fighter was upright, but one whole side looked as if it had been peeled back. You could see right to the inside. The left engine pod was cranked out at a sharp angle.

Ax was inside the fighter. He lowered his head to peer at me through the hole in the fighter's side. <Prince Jake. I'm glad you're all right.>

"I'm glad I'm all right, too," I said. "Now . . . where are we?"

"*Where* is easy," Cassie said. "Rain forest. Not Africa, because I've seen monkeys with prehensile tails. You know, tails they can swing by. Most likely, we're in Central or South America. Either the Costa Rican rain forest, or the Amazon rain forest."

"I'm betting Amazon," Marco said brightly. "I'm also taking bets on whether we live long enough for me to collect on bets."

I laughed. "You're always such an optimist, Marco."

I turned back to Cassie. "So. Amazon rain forest, huh?"

"Like I said, the question of *where* we are is fairly easy."

"Cassie, why do I have the feeling there's something you're not telling me?" I asked her.

"Remember when we were in orbit? Remember how it was night in North America, but the sun was just coming up over the Red Sea?"

I shrugged. "I guess so."

"Well, after we fired at the Blade ship, as we were going down it was daylight here. Over South America."

It took me a few seconds to realize what she was talking about.

Ax came trotting out of the Bug fighter. He wiped his hands on a rag. <Thanks to Cassie's observation, it seems pretty clear that when we and the Blade ship fired simultaneously and the Dracon beams intersected, we created what we call a *Sario Rip*.>

"A what? A *Sario Rip*? What's that?"

<We blew a small hole in space-time. And were drawn in through that hole.>

"English, please," I warned. "Plain English, please."

"We were blown through time, Jake," Cassie

said. "We aren't *where* we want to be. And we aren't *when* we want to be."

I stared at her. "Did we go forwards or back? Are we in the past or the future?"

<Yes,> Ax said. <It's definitely one of those two choices.>

Chapter 12

1:22 P.M. Again.

"So let me just summarize here. We are probably in the Amazon rain forest. And we are either in our own past, or in our own future. We have no way to fly this Bug fighter out of here. We have no way of knowing if there's a city or town or even a road near here." I looked around at my friends. "Anyone have anything to add?"

<I know that it is one twenty-two p.m.,> Ax said. <I just don't know what day or year it is.>

Andalites have the ability to keep track of time naturally. Like some kind of internal clock. It's useful. Of course, it's more useful if you know what century you're in.

Cassie held up her hand, like she was in school. "The rain forest is full of poisonous snakes, poisonous insects, poisonous plants, and poisonous frogs."

"Excuse me?" Marco said. "Poisonous frogs? Did you say poisonous *frogs*?"

"Plus, there is at least one large predator: the jaguar."

"Love their cars," Marco said.

"Right now we have no food and no water," Rachel added helpfully. "Also, no weapons."

<Why do we need weapons?> Tobias asked. <Morph into birds and we'll just fly out of here.>

"None of us can stay in morph for more than two hours," Cassie pointed out. "Realistically, we can't fly more than forty or fifty kilometres an hour at best. That's maybe a hundred kilometres per morph. And we could be a thousand kilometres from nowhere."

"Besides," Marco said glumly. "What are we supposed to do? Find a town, make a reverse charge call to our families and tell them we're in South America? 'Hey, Dad, guess what? I'm in Brazil. Or maybe Costa Rica. Could you come and pick me up?'"

"If there even *is* a town," Rachel said. "If there even *are* phones. If our parents have been born yet, or are still alive. You're kind of missing something — we may be in the year two thousand BC. Or . . . we might be in the year AD ten thousand."

"Ax, what's the deal with this *Sario Rip*?" I

asked the Andalite. "I mean, is there some way to undo it?"

Ax didn't answer. Instead, I noticed his stalk eyes turning slowly to his right. <We are not alone,> Ax said.

I shot a glance in the direction Ax was looking. Something moved! I had a fleeting impression of a shoulder, arm and head.

<Humanoid,> Ax said. <I didn't see it very well. But it was watching us.>

"Swell," I said. "Tobias?"

<I'm on it,> he said, opening his wings and flapping away through the trees.

<As for the *Sario Rip*, I . . . all I know is what it is. It's a rip in space-time.>

"Yeah, you told us that," Marco said.

<I think. . .> Ax hung his head. <Prince Jake, we studied the *Sario Rip* effect in school. But there was a game later that day. And I was thinking more about the game than class. Also, there was this female who distracted me.>

Marco laughed. "Ax, are you telling us you were too busy flirting with some girl to pay attention to the lesson?"

Ax didn't answer. He just said, <I don't exactly know whether you can reverse a *Sario Rip*. I remember some things, but not everything.>

"I'm thirsty," Rachel said. "Whatever else we're going to do, we have to find water. And food. Ax, can we fix the Bug fighter?"

<We can fly with just one engine,> Ax said. <The ripped skin of the craft is irrelevant as long as we stay in the atmosphere and fly slow. But the effects of the *Sario Rip* have wiped out the ship's software. It's been erased.>

"Can you rewrite the software?" Rachel asked.

<Yes. But it would take me twenty years, at least.>

"Better and better," I said. "Hey. Wait. What happened to the Blade ship?"

Ax looked blank.

"I saw it going down along with us," Cassie said. "But I didn't see it crash."

"So maybe, in addition to everything else, we have Visser Three and a shipload of Hork-Bajir warriors to worry about," I said. "Someone please give me some good news."

"Well, it's still daylight," Marco said, putting on a big phoney grin. "When night falls, then we'll be—"

<Jake! Duck!> Tobias yelled.

For once in my life, I didn't stop to think about it. I ducked. And even as I ducked, I saw the face. I saw the arm. I saw the spear.

It was coming straight at me.

Right for my face.

The vision! It was the hallucination!

I ducked. The spear went over my head and flew on harmlessly into the bush.

Tobias flapped wildly into the air. <I

shouldn't have been resting,> he berated himself. <I should have been in the air.>

I was too weirded out to worry about Tobias. "I knew that was going to happen," I said. "That spear. The kid who threw it. I knew!"

Cassie looked strangely at me. "Jake, what are you—"

<Three people,> Tobias interrupted. <They almost look like they might be kids. They're hauling butt out of here. Which is what we'd better think about doing, too.>

"Why?" Rachel demanded indignantly. "We can handle some kids with spears."

<Forget the kids. I see a group of twenty . . . maybe thirty Hork-Bajir. They're tearing up the forest and coming this way!>

"We can't leave the Bug fighter!" Rachel protested. "How else are we going to get out of here?"

"We can't stand and fight twenty Hork-Bajir warriors, either," I said. "We have to pull back."

I glanced over and saw Cassie. She had retrieved the spear from the bushes. It was a long, thin stick. There was no spearhead on it. It was just a sharp stick with the sharp end blackened.

"That doesn't look too deadly," I said.

Cassie shook her head. "No. You probably couldn't kill much with this stick. Unless the tip was dipped in poison. And we are in the home office of natural poisons."

"The local people . . . I guess they wouldn't

waste their time using a weapon that didn't work, would they?" I said.

"No," Cassie said flatly. "The chances are pretty good that this spear is poison-tipped. There are poisonous frogs and plants down here that are used for arrow and spear poison. Very deadly. Very, *very* deadly. The Hork-Bajir are definitely not our only problem."

<Jake, you guys need to move out,> Tobias warned. He was overhead again. I couldn't see him, but I knew he was up above the jungle canopy. <I can't see well enough through all this foliage. But I think a group of Hork-Bajir is getting close to you.>

Decision time. Stay and fight? We'd lose. Run away? We'd be giving up the Bug fighter, our only way home.

"Ax? Is there something . . . *anything* . . . you can take out of the Bug fighter that would make it impossible for the Yeerks to fly it?"

Ax stared at me with his main eyes, even as his stalk eyes swept the forest around us. <Yes. Yes, I can think of something.>

"Then get it," I said.

<Jake! There's no time,> Tobias called down. He must have been close enough to hear me. But the foliage was so dense I had no clear idea where he was.

Ax hesitated, not sure what to do.

The others all looked at me.

"Do it, Ax," I said. He raced for the Bug

fighter. "Everyone else, get out of here."

"I'm staying with you," Rachel protested.

"I'm not staying. Minimum risk," I snapped. "We only need Ax to handle this. No point risking anyone else."

I plunged into the green. I grabbed Rachel's arm and pulled her along. Cassie and Marco followed me.

<Jake,> Tobias called down. <If Ax isn't out of there in under two minutes, he's not going to get out of there.>

I didn't answer.

It's the worst thing about being a so-called leader — the times when you take a risk with someone else's life. If Ax ended up dead, it was going to be very hard to explain to my friends.

And to myself.

Chapter 13

1:48 P.M.

I can't begin to explain what the rain forest is like. To explain it, you'd have to be a poet and a scientist and a horror writer.

All I can say is how it makes you feel. You feel small. Tiny. Alone. Hopelessly weak. Afraid.

You feel heat and suffocating humidity. It's like there's not enough air. Every breath is like sucking air through a straw. You're breathing steam and perfume and the stink of dying, rotting things.

The jungle is all around you. It presses against you on all sides. Wet leaves in your face; creepers that seem to reach up to trip you; sharp-edged stalks that cut you.

And then there are the twin horrors: bugs and thirst.

Mosquitoes, gnats, big flies and other flying insects I didn't even have names for followed us in swirling clouds. They'd descend and attack, then disappear for no reason, only to attack again later. If you stopped, even for a few seconds, you could find your foot covered with ants or centipedes or beetles or bugs that defied description.

And it didn't help that we were shoe-less.

The heat sucked every gramme of moisture out of us. It was as bad as any desert. You'd think with all the greenery there would be water everywhere. But no. The actual ground under our feet was dry. All the water is captured in the plants.

All the while, as we fought our way through the thickets of vines and ferns and bushes and gnats and flies and mosquitoes, we were followed by a serenade of cackles, groans, screams, yelps, insane animal giggles, clicking, scratching and the occasional coughing roar as each new species commented on the idiocy of a bunch of suburban kids wandering around the rain forest. For all we knew, they were taking bets on how long the dumb humans would survive.

We had pushed two hundred metres deeper into the rain forest from the Bug fighter when we heard an uproar behind us.

"Andalite!" a Hork-Bajir voice bellowed.

"Andalite!"

<They're after him!> Tobias called down from above. <Ax has six Hork-Bajir on his tail! You happy now, Jake? Ax-man! Look out! Behind you!>

I bit my lip till I tasted my own blood.

"We have to morph and go back for him," Rachel said. Her eyes were blazing.

I could have said no. I had reasons to say no. We were in an unknown place, facing lousy odds. Besides, of us all, Ax was the fastest and best able to escape. But Rachel would have just gone anyway.

"Just two of us go," I snapped. "Me and you, Rachel. Marco and Cassie, stay back."

"Why are we staying back?" Marco asked, outraged.

"Because we need backup, Marco," I said tersely.

I don't know if he understood this or not. Rachel did. She started to morph.

I was morphing into my tiger morph as fast as I could. Rachel was already well into her grizzly bear morph — massive shoulders and shaggy brown fur and long, curved claws.

TSEEEWWW! TSEEEWWW!

The sound of Dracon beams reached us. The jungle animals up in the trees exploded in a fury of commentary.

Ke-RRRRAAAAAWWWW!

HOO! HOOHOOHOOHOO!

I could hear something large crashing around the brush, but I couldn't see anything. In the rain forest you're lucky if you can see two metres in any direction.

<I'm ready,> Rachel said.

<Wait for me,> I told her.

<Catch up when you can,> Rachel snapped. She lumbered away, back towards the Bug fighter, a huge, rolling mass of heavy fur and muscle. I cursed her silently.

My body was already covered with orange-and-black-striped fur. I was on all fours. Long, yellow fangs grew in my mouth. Long, wicked claws grew where my fingernails had been.

I felt the tiger's mind.

I saw through the tiger's eyes.

I felt the surge of power, the rush of the tiger's might. He was at home in a tropical forest. This was the kind of place he belonged. The tiger was lord of his own native turf.

But of course in the tiger's native jungles, there aren't Hork-Bajir. And there's no Visser Three.

I leaped forward, following the path Rachel had ploughed through the bushes. I caught up with her easily. I belonged in the jungle. The grizzly did not. Rachel was breathing hard.

<I can't see . . . can't find them . . . keep hearing noises, but they keep moving.>

I listened with my tiger's ears. I receded just a bit within the tiger mind and let the animal instincts guide me. The tiger knew how to follow sounds in the rain forest.

<Come on, Rachel,> I said. I plunged forwards, towards where I heard the loudest sounds crashing through the forest. But I soon realized Rachel couldn't keep up.

I was really annoyed right then. At Rachel, for being so impulsive. At Tobias for acting like I *wanted* to put Ax in danger. At the Yeerks for causing all this. At the jungle itself. And worst of all, at me.

I'd made mistakes. Too many mistakes. Now I had to choose. Stay with Rachel, or rush ahead and try to find Ax.

Help came from the sky. <Left about fifteen metres, Jake,> Tobias called down to me.

I was mad at Tobias. But not so mad I would ignore him. I charged left, slinking swiftly through the brush.

<Jake! Look out! There's one right—>

"Haarrgghh!" the Hork-Bajir yelled triumphantly. He swung a bladed arm at me and sliced through the ferns and bushes like a lawn mower going through grass.

His elbow blade missed me by centimetres. I felt the breeze from it.

I knew what to do next. I fired the coiled muscles in my hind legs and I flew. In mid-air I extended my paws, each as wide as a frying pan. Out came my claws.

And I roared. HRRROOOOOWWWWRRRR!

I swear, that sound actually silenced the monkeys and birds.

I hit the Hork-Bajir. He went down, swinging fast, but too slow. Hork-Bajir are fast. But when it comes to close-in work, slashing and parrying and applying the teeth, the tiger is faster and nastier.

He slashed. I felt pain sear my right shoulder.

I slashed and heard the Hork-Bajir cry out.

His snake-head jerked fast, aiming his forehead blades for my face.

I ducked and dived in, sinking my teeth into his neck.

From somewhere I heard the sound of a bear's pained roar. I heard crashing, thudding sounds.

I pulled back, leaving the deadly, bladed, two-metre-tall Hork-Bajir lying on the jungle floor, moaning in pain.

I actually felt a moment of pity. The Hork-Bajir race has been enslaved by the Yeerks. This Hork-Bajir warrior didn't ask to be here, bleeding from a dozen wounds in an alien jungle a billion kilometres from his home.

But then, I didn't ask to be here, either.

I listened for sounds of Ax. Nothing.

I listened for Hork-Bajir. Nothing.

I listened for Rachel. Nothing.

It was like they'd all just disappeared in the green. Green, everywhere I looked.

Then. . .

A sharp pain in my left paw. I looked at the Hork-Bajir, but no, he hadn't moved.

I realized I was falling over.

Simply falling over.

Out of the corner of my eye, I saw the snake slithering off. It was bright yellow.

<Demorph!> I told myself. <Demorph!>

But my head was swimming. And the green was closing in around me. Burying me in green.

A bird landed beside me. I could see that.

<Jake! Morph back, man! Morph back!>

I was trying. I was trying to remember what it was I was supposed to become. Then. . .

Flash!

I was walking home from school. Me and Marco.

We were talking, wondering what Tobias wanted.

Tobias's thought-speak voice was in our heads saying —

Flash!

Tobias's voice saying, <That's it, Jake. Come on, man. Keep at it.>

I could see again! I could see my hands

89

stretched out in front of me on the ground. They were half-human, half-tiger.

Could I morph away from poison? Would morphing get it out of my system? Should have asked Ax, I berated myself.

But I was already learning the answer. As I became more human, I felt the poison weaken.

<Come on, Jake, come on,> Tobias said. <There's no time!>

"What . . . what is it? More Hork-Bajir?" I asked him when I had a human mouth again.

<No. It's Rachel.>

I felt my heart miss several beats. I climbed up, rickety from the quick change. I felt like throwing up. Maybe it was the poison. Maybe it was just too much happening at once. "Where is she?" I asked.

<Straight behind you. Maybe thirty metres. Hurry! I'll go up and see what's happening.>

He flapped away, leaving me alone and barefoot and vulnerable in the rain forest.

I found Rachel by following the damage she had done: three Hork-Bajir lying unconscious or worse. I didn't have time to worry about them.

Because that's when I saw Rachel.

She was out cold, still in grizzly morph. She'd been cut up badly by Hork-Bajir blades.

She was lying there on her side, bleeding. But that's not what made me want to scream.

Her fur was alive.

Alive with a million ants that were already ripping away a million tiny bites from her wounded flesh.

Chapter 14

"Rachel!" I yelled. "Wake up!"

<Jake! Stop shouting,> Tobias warned from up above me. <Hork-Bajir could still be all around here! I can't see through all this undergrowth.>

I threw myself down next to Rachel and started swatting at the ants. But instead of getting rid of them, the ants just swarmed across my hands.

There had to be ten thousand ants. Rachel had fallen almost on top of their mound. I could see ants carrying away tiny pieces of bloody bear flesh.

"Do you know if there is any water near here?" I asked Tobias.

<There's a stream. But it's too far. Jake, she weighs hundreds of kilogrammes. What are you

92

going to do, carry her to the water?>

I could see Rachel's bear chest rising and falling. She was breathing. Still alive. I kicked her. I kicked her hard. "Wake up!" I hissed. "Come on, Rachel, wake up!"

The ants were getting at her ears now. They swarmed across her closed eyes. I wanted to scream. I wanted to cry.

I don't think I've ever felt so totally helpless. Rachel was out cold. The thousands of swarming ants would make sure she never woke up. They would kill the bear before Rachel could morph out. They would eat out her eyes and crawl into her head, and there was nothing I could do.

"Tobias! More ants! Find more ants!"

<Are you nuts?>

"Do it!" I yelled, not even caring if someone heard me. "I need another colony of ants!"

Tobias clicked. I could see his fierce eyes grow wider. He flapped away, staying as low to the ground as he could. He circled tightly, and then flared to kill his speed.

<Here! Here!> he yelled.

At that moment I heard movement in the bushes. I looked and saw two wolves. Two very out-of-place wolves. Their intelligent faces were sticking out of the brush.

"Cassie! Marco! That is you two, right?"

Looking closer, I could see that they had

been in a fight. There were cuts. There was blood. They began to demorph.

<Oh, my God,> Cassie moaned as she saw Rachel and realized what was happening.

I didn't have time to explain. I bent down and began yanking out tufts of bloody grizzly bear fur.

<What are you doing? Leave her alone!> Marco yelled.

I yanked several handfuls of bloody fur. Then I raced towards the spot where Tobias waited. He was resting on a strong fern, looking down at a swarming mound of ants.

I took a small sample of the grizzly fur and laid it right beside the mouth of the ant mound.

The reaction was instantaneous. Hundreds of ants swarmed across the bloody fur.

I used another tuft of fur to lift a handful of ants, then I walked a metre towards Rachel and dropped the tuft. I repeated the process, getting closer and closer to Rachel. I was worried the ants might lose the scent. But they were keeping up with me, and even racing ahead.

Slowly, surely, I led the ants to Rachel.

Cassie and Marco were human once more. They looked like I probably looked: scared, horrified, vulnerable.

"We have to get them off her!" Cassie cried when she saw me. "They're inside her ears! They're in her mouth! They'll kill her!"

"I know." I _____ped my last blood-soaked tuft of fur. If t____ didn't work, Rachel was finished.

I stepped asi___ ___nd put my arm around Cassie.

The new colony ____ants followed the trail I'd left them. There ____ a moment's hesitation, almost as if the wh___ ___ampaging colony paused upon seeing the be___

But then, like ____ ____well-trained army they were, they attacke____ ___n thousand new ants swarmed on to Rach___ ___nconscious body. They slammed into a wall o___ ___ts from the first colony.

I've been an ant___ ____e seen how different colonies of ants get a ___ ___. I hoped they would act in the same way h___

They did. It was ____ ____some old Civil War battle. The two armie____ ____arged at each other. Perfect, obedient auto___ ___ns responding only to smell and instinct.

They attacked each o___ ___. The ants swarmed back out of Rachel's ea___ ___d mouth, ready for the battle.

"That was good think___ ____Jake," Cassie said. "But sooner or later, one ____ ___ny will win."

"We have to hope Rac___ ____egains conscious-ness before then," I said.

The enemy armies of ar___ ___attled ferociously. It wouldn't look like much ____ ___nost people. But having been an ant, I ha___ ____me idea of the awesome slaughter that was going on in the fur of the grizzly.

Down there, ants were being torn apart by other ants. Literally torn apart. Legs ripped out. Heads bitten off. Stinging poisons being sprayed.

The battle was turning. The challengers' mound was too far away. They weren't able to call up enough reinforcements. In a few minutes the desperate ant war would be over.

But while they fought, they did not tear into Rachel's flesh. And then. . .

<Unh . . . wha . . . oh! Oh! Oh! I'm covered in ants!>

"Rachel! Rachel! It's me, Jake. Morph out. Morph out and be ready to run!"

Rachel didn't have to be told twice. She started demorphing. She shrank. Pink flesh replaced fur. Massive shoulders and huge paws became smaller, human features.

"Oh!" Rachel cried as soon as she had a human mouth. "Arrrrggghh!"

"Rachel, get up! Follow me!" I said to her. "Tobias? Where's that stream?"

Tobias rose up and flew swiftly through the trees. I followed, crashing through the bushes, my bare feet torn, tripping. It was no more than thirty metres. It felt like a kilometre.

Rachel was screaming now. Rachel is the bravest person I know. But the thousands of vicious ants were beginning to attack her, now that they were done attacking each other. No one can stand that.

No one can stand that.

"Get off me! Oh, no! Oh! They're in my—"

Suddenly there was no more green. A muddy stream . . . I leaped for the water. Pah-LOOSH!

I heard Rachel hit the water beside me. Pah-LOOSH!

I swam towards her. She was still under-water. The water was too murky for me to be able to see her well. All I saw was flailing limbs.

Ants were floating to the surface of the water and being carried away by the current.

Then. . .

SPLOOSH!

Rachel came up, gasping for air.

"Are you OK?" I asked her.

She looked around, confused for a moment. Then she recognized me. And she spotted Marco and Cassie on the bank of the stream.

"Get out of the water!" Cassie screamed.

I grabbed Rachel's arm and dragged her towards the bank. I pushed her ahead of me, slipping and sliding up through the muddy grass. I was just pulling my feet up out of the water when I saw the churning, frothing commotion Cassie had seen first.

I yanked my feet away, just ahead of a school of flesh-eating piranha.

97

"This is the rain forest?" Rachel demanded angrily, spitting water and combing through her hair for any remaining ants. "*This* is the rain forest everyone wants to save? Ants and piranhas and snakes and bugs the size of rats? Well, as far as I'm concerned they can burn it down, pave it over, and put up malls and supermarkets!"

I sat staring at the piranhas. They say a school of piranha can strip a cow down to nothing but bones in a few minutes.

Right then, thinking about what almost happened, shaking and panting and wanting to cry, I agreed with Rachel.

Chapter 15

"Now we need to find Ax," I said. "But we need to be careful. This jungle alone is enough to mess us up badly. And we have the Yeerks to deal with as well."

<I am not lost, Prince Jake,> a thought-speak voice said.

"Ax!" I cried.

<Yes, it's me,> Ax said. <But I am in a morph. Don't be startled.> With that, he dropped from the tree above us and landed on the ground.

"Well," Marco commented with great satisfaction. "Someone finally made a monkey out of Ax."

He was small, covered in brown fur, and definitely a monkey. But he was alive.

I don't think I've ever felt so relieved in my life. I had been screwing up plenty. First by

99

deciding to go into the stupid Safeway to begin with, then by endangering Tobias, then by endangering Ax, then by leaving Rachel alone to almost get killed. But at least no one had got killed.

Yet.

"I'm thinking spider monkey," Cassie said, frowning. "But I'm not sure. I'm not all that strong on rain forest animals."

The monkey — Ax — was holding something in his paw. It was bright yellow and about the size of a computer diskette, only round and a little thicker.

"What is that?" I asked.

<I did what you told me to do,> Ax said. <This is a vital part of the Bug fighter — the computer core. No one can fly the Bug fighter without it.>

<That thing is the computer?> Tobias asked.

<Yes, the Yeerks are still somewhat primitive. An Andalite version would be a third this size.>

"Well, I'm relieved you're OK, Ax," I said. "We haven't been doing very well."

<I barely made it,> Ax said simply. <There are several dozen Hork-Bajir out combing the forest, looking for us. I think they are divided now into platoons of five, each accompanied by a human-Controller. I haven't seen the Visser, but he will be around as well. And as you know,

Visser Three can morph, so he could be any of the animals we see.>

"That's a good point," Rachel said. "We have to be on the lookout for animals as well as Hork-Bajir and the natives."

"The human-Controllers," Marco said thoughtfully. "I think I know why they're travelling with the Hork-Bajir. See, the human-Controllers would know which animals belong here in the rain forest, and which don't. If they see a grizzly bear or a tiger or a wolf, they'll know that it doesn't belong. They'll know it's us."

"Good thinking, Marco. We need local morphs," I said.

<I can take you to the monkeys,> Ax suggested. <I believe they are close relatives of yours.>

"Marco is second cousin to a monkey," Rachel said.

I was glad to see she was teasing Marco again. It meant she was back. Still, there was a darkness in her eyes. Not even Rachel could just shake off what she'd been through. And knowing Rachel, she would react by being more aggressive. Maybe too aggressive.

"Monkeys would be good," Cassie said. "It would get us up off the ground and into the trees."

"OK, Ax, lead on. Tobias? I hate to ask, but we could use some air cover."

<No problem,> Tobias said.

He flew up into the trees. I knew he was tired. And I knew he was hungry. Flying is hard work, and a bird's metabolism is fast. They can't endure long periods of hunger as well as a human. But what else could I do?

Ax did not lead us very far. Within ten minutes we were standing beneath a group of monkeys chittering and yipping in the trees high above us.

It isn't possible to acquire a morph from a person who's morphed. In other words, we couldn't just copy Ax's monkey morph. We had to go to an actual monkey.

<I believe I can get one of them to come down,> Ax said.

"How?" Marco asked.

Ax hesitated. It's hard to tell if a monkey is embarrassed, let alone a monkey with an Andalite mind. But I could have sworn Ax was embarrassed.

<I . . . I believe that I am — that is to say my morph is — an attractive female. One of the males seemed interested earlier.>

"Well, that does it," Marco said flatly. "We have moved permanently to bizarre-o world. We've travelled in time, we're in a jungle fighting brain-stealing aliens and ten thousand annoying species of bugs, and our resident space cadet is a hot-looking monkey. Somebody—"

"— wake me up when we get back to reality."

"— wake me up when we get back to reality."

Marco and I said it at the same moment. He stared at me. I stared at him. Everyone else stared at us.

I sighed. "I guess I have something to tell you guys. I should have said something earlier, probably. But I thought I was just going nuts or something. See, I've been having these flashes. Really intense. It's like, I'd be in school and then suddenly I was here. And since we got here, I've been having flashes that I'm back home."

Rachel rolled her eyes as if to say, "What next?" Cassie looked concerned. Marco looked like he was trying to find a joke in the situation, but was too tired to come up with anything.

"I knew what Marco was going to say just now because that was one of the flashes," I said.

Ax stared at me with large monkey eyes. <Prince Jake, how long ago did you start having these flashbacks?>

I shrugged. "It was just this afternoon. Yesterday, or today, whatever you'd call it. I was square dancing when the first one happened. Why?"

"*You* were square dancing?" Marco said. "I'd

have paid to see that."

Ax scratched his neck vigorously, then looked intently at what he'd scratched up. He popped whatever it was into his mouth. Obviously, he was letting the monkey mind have some control. <Prince Jake, as I said, I'm not an expert on *Sario Rips*. But I think what's happening is that the flashbacks are fluctuations where two simultaneous identical states of consciousness intersect outside of space-time."

"That would have been my guess," Marco said. "Simultaneous . . . whatevers."

<I have a theory. . .> Ax began.

"A theory is more than I have. What is it?"

<I suspect we have moved backwards in time. But not far. We are existing simultaneously both here and back at home. There are now two Marcos, two Cassies, two of each of us. One here, one there. At the same time. The flashbacks only started today. So I suspect we have gone back one day in time, a little less.>

"That's good," Marco said.

<No,> Ax said solemnly. <It's not good. We are in two places at the same time. That is impossible. It's a time-space anomaly. It's an unstable condition.>

"Meaning. . . ?" I pressed.

<I think it means that the two groups, the two Marcos, Rachels, and so ons, will annihilate each other. Like matter and anti-matter, it is not

possible for there to be two of us in the same time.>

"So why haven't we annihilated ourselves yet?" Rachel asked.

<We are still within the *Sario Rip* effect,> Ax said. <I think. So . . . so I think we're OK till we get back to the time when the rip occurred. At that time, the rip will end, and we'll have an impossible situation: two identical groups of people existing in two places at one time. I think my teacher said it would cause a mutual annihilation. We'd cease to exist. Both groups. Here and back home. The time when the *Sario Rip* occurred was eight fifty-four, exactly.>

"In other words, if we're getting back to our own time, we have to do it before the *Sario Rip* occurs at eight fifty-four," I said.

<Yes. We'd have to go back and change the time line. So that none of this would happen. We have less than six hours.>

"How do we do that?"

<I'm not sure.>

I nodded. "Well, if we're trapped, so is Visser Three, right? He must know about *Sario Rips*, too. If he's going back, we can go back with him. All we have to do is get to the Blade ship, hide out on board, and let Visser Three take us home. I mean, that's the only way, right?"

<There could be—> Ax started to say. Then he stopped.

"What?" I asked him. "Is there some other way to get back?"

Ax gave me a long look. Like he wasn't quite sure what to say. Or whether to say anything at all. He was in monkey morph, so I couldn't read his expression.

<As I said, Prince Jake, I wasn't paying attention the day they taught this in school.>

I knew he was hiding something. I should have pressed him. But I didn't.

Just one more mistake from the "fearless leader" of the Animorphs.

Chapter 16

It was easy to "acquire" the monkeys. Several of them swung down from the tree to sniff at Ax. And they didn't seem terribly frightened by any of us, since we were all standing very still and quiet.

I reached very slowly, very gently for one particular monkey. He looked at my hand, considering it. Then he turned his back, as if asking me to scratch it.

"OK," I said. "I'd be glad to."

I scratched the little monkey's back. And as I did, I closed my eyes and focused my thoughts on the monkey. He became quiet, like he was in a trance. That's how animals usually are when they're being acquired.

I absorbed the monkey DNA into me.

"This should be especially easy," Cassie

commented as she finished acquiring a different monkey. "These monkeys aren't direct relatives of *Homo sapiens*, but still, most of our DNA will be identical. After all, a chimpanzee's DNA is like ninety-seven per cent identical to human DNA."

"Or in Marco's case, ninety-nine point nine per cent," Rachel interjected.

"Yes, it's like the fact that Rachel's DNA is actually ninety-nine per cent identical to Malibu Barbie," Marco shot back.

"Could we concentrate here?" I said gruffly. Actually, I was relieved to see everyone behaving normally. It's when Cassie isn't talking about animals and Marco and Rachel aren't teasing each other that you have to worry.

"Ax? Did you have any problems with the monkey's mind when you morphed?" Cassie asked.

<No. Except . . . well, they are similar to morphing a human, but much more excitable. Also, they don't fall over as easily as humans do.>

Ax is constantly amazed that humans walk around on just two legs, without even a tail to hold us up.

"OK, let's do it," I said. "We're short on time, and we are exposed, sitting out here looking like dumb, barefoot kids from the suburbs. Tobias? Ax? Both of you keep an eye out for any trouble."

<This whole rain forest is nothing but trouble,> Tobias said darkly. <Especially when you're a red-tailed hawk and you stick out like a sore thumb.>

He was right, but I had to worry about one thing at a time. And I knew from my "visions" that we could successfully morph into monkeys. Unfortunately, the visions didn't tell me whether we'd succeed or fail, end up alive . . . or not.

I concentrated on a mental image of the monkey. And very, very quickly, I began to feel the changes.

The real monkeys began to see the changes, too.

SQUEEE! SQUEEE! SQUEEE!

The real monkeys leaped on to the tree trunk and scampered up towards the high branches.

I shrank. That was to be expected. But the more I shrank, the more vulnerable I felt. Brown fur sprouted from my arms and legs. My face remained furless, and my lips puffed out to form a rubbery muzzle.

The largest single change was the tail. I felt it come shooting out from the base of my spine. But I'd had a tail before, so I didn't think much about it.

Then I realized something. The tail moved. Not just back and forth, like a dog's tail. It moved like a fifth arm.

<Hey, the tail is neat,> Cassie said. <Try

moving it. You can feel that there's a part of your brain that controls it. Just like an extra hand.>

She was right. And Ax was right, too. There was very little that was new or strange inside the monkey's mind. Like a human, it had only a few basic instincts. Like a human, it depended on learning to guide its actions.

The eyes were similar to human eyes. The ears no better than our own. The sense of smell was a bit improved, though.

<That was an easy morph,> Rachel said. <So. What can this monkey do?>

I shrugged my narrow monkey shoulders. <I guess it climbs trees.>

I turned to the tree trunk. Like almost all the rain forest trees, it was shockingly tall. And there were no low branches. But there were strangling vines wrapped all around the trunk, like a nest of snakes.

<Let's try it out,> I said. I reached for a vine and held it tentatively. I positioned one foot. Then I carefully reached for another handhold.

<Prince Jake,> Ax said. <Let the creature do the climbing. It knows how. Like this.>

He put the Bug fighter's computer in his mouth and leaped right through the air, snatched a handhold, and was twenty metres up the tree before I could blink three times.

I took a deep breath and relaxed my control. I allowed the monkey mind to come forward and just said, <Climb.>

Ax was right. The monkey knew how to climb. You know the way Michael Jordan knows his way around a basketball court? Or the way Kristi Yamaguchi knows her way around the ice rink? That's how the monkey knew the trees. It knew the trees. It understood the trees. It was born to be in the trees.

Hands, toes, hands, toes, it found every little handhold, every foothold, never a hesitation, never a doubt, never a question. That monkey knew exactly, precisely what to do.

I felt like I had swallowed ten Mountain Dews and a box of Ring-Dings. I was tiny, but man, I had energy. I flew up that tree.

I met Cassie up in the high canopy. <Yow! Ax was right. This monkey can climb trees!>

<That's not all it can do,> she said. The others were just catching up to us. <Watch this.>

She launched herself out into the air.

We were twenty metres up, easy, as high as a five-storey building, and Cassie just fired her hind legs and flew through the air.

She snatched a hanging vine with one hand, but never stopped swinging forward.

That was all I needed to see. It was a game of chase through the treetops. The monkey wanted to play, and so did I. I needed some fun. I needed some fun in the worst way.

I leaped. For about two seconds that felt like

ten minutes, I hung in the air. Then, my left hand simply reached out, found a branch, swung me forwards, launched me once again through the air, reached out again. . .

Swing and fly and grab and swing and fly and grab!

<Oh, yes! Oh, definitely!> Marco exulted as he followed Cassie and me through the trees.

Swing! Flyyyyy! Catch! Swing! Flyyyyy! Catch!

The little monkey brain processed every move, prepared every action and reaction. The entire world was branches and vines to the monkey.

Swing! Fly through the air with the ground a deadly twenty metres down! Catch at the last possible second! Swing again, out into the void, catch just in time to save your life!

It was the scene from my flash. Me, zipping through the trees.

Ax paused to let us all catch up. He wrapped his tail around a branch and hung there, panting. I wrapped my own tail around the branch and let go with my hands and feet. I hung there, high above the forest floor, by my tail. I swayed gently in the breeze.

<This sounds weird, but there's something . . . familiar about this,> I said to Cassie when she caught up with us. <I mean, not to the monkey, but to me. To me, the human.>

<It's called brachiating, I think,> Cassie

said. <Swinging through the trees. It's what our distant ancestors did, millions of years ago. Maybe little bits of that memory are still stuck in the back of our human brains. Maybe all the stages of evolution are still a part of us.>

<Or maybe it just reminds me of playing on jungle gyms when I was a little kid.>

<Oh, sure, if you want the boring, *obvious* explanation,> Cassie said with a laugh.

<It's like gymnastics,> Rachel said. <Only this monkey could totally destroy any human on the uneven parallel bars. If the monkey team could be in the Olympics, they'd win every medal.>

<Can I ask a question?> Ax interrupted. <Where are we going?>

We all stared at him. Then we burst out laughing. The monkey bodies laughed, too, a wild, chittering sound. That just made us laugh all the more.

<I guess we did get kind of carried away,> I said to Ax. <Now get serious. We have stuff to do. We have to find the Blade ship. And we have to get back to our own time before eight fifty-four.>

<Can we play chase some more first?> Marco asked.

And I would have said yes, because I was as caught up as he was in the idiot joy of being a monkey.

Chapter 17

4:32 P.M.

I don't think I'd ever realized how strong Hork-Bajir are till we followed them as they rampaged through the rain forest.

They used their arm blades to slash at the vegetation, leaving a path of destruction in their wake. They slashed and slashed and never seemed to tire.

There was a human-Controller with them. A guy who looked like he might be nineteen or twenty. He was in good shape, but he was gasping and sweating and struggling to keep up with the powerful, tireless Hork-Bajir.

Far above them we swung and flew and caught and swung again.

<Are these guys going somewhere, or just wandering around?> Rachel grumbled. <Tick-

115

tock, ticktock. We're running out of time.>

"There! There!" the human-Controller rasped weakly, pointing in the direction of the base of the tree we were in. "That animal! That pig-like thing. I don't think it belongs here."

I think the guy was just tired. Looking for an excuse to sit down and rest. But without pausing even to consider, the lead Hork-Bajir drew his Dracon beam and fired.

Tseeewww!

The wild pig, or whatever it was, sizzled and disappeared. The Dracon beam kept travelling. It hit and sliced through the trunk of our tree.

<Move!> I yelled as the tree began to shudder and sway.

We leaped wildly for the next tree. I fired myself out into the air. The tree was falling too fast. No time to plan a landing!

I flew through the air for a very, very long two seconds. I dropped. The ground came rushing up. I could see the face of the human-Controller staring up at me, wondering. . .

A branch! I reached. Missed!

No, wait! Suddenly I was stopping, swinging in a crazy circle. I almost laughed when I realized what had happened. My tail had grabbed the branch my hand had missed.

"I don't like that monkey," the human-Controller said.

The Hork-Bajir leader once again drew his

Dracon beam and aimed for me.

But I was out of there. I raced back along the branch, holding on with my toes. And I swung around the back of the trunk a split second ahead of. . .

TSEEWWW!

ZZZZAAAPPP! The tree trunk exploded right in front of me as the Dracon beam turned its sap to steam. Heat scorched my face. I lost my hold and began to fall.

Then . . . a hand grabbed me.

<Hold on!> Rachel said as she swung me towards a new branch.

"That does it! That's no real monkey," the human-Controller yelled. "The monkeys! Kill all the monkeys! Kill every monkey you see!"

Five Hork-Bajir drew their weapons.

<No!> Cassie cried. <Jake! We have to stop them!>

<Cassie, get out of here! Go!> I yelled.

TSEEEWWW! TSEEEWWW! TSEEEWWW!

Dracon beams fired their killing light. Tree branches fell away like someone was trimming a rose bush. And one of the beams hit a monkey.

<Cassie! Marco! Ax!> I yelled.

<It wasn't one of us,> Marco answered.

Monkeys were destroyed. Birds in the trees were destroyed. A sloth and its baby, hanging from a branch, were destroyed. The Hork-Bajir were on a rampage. They were past just shooting at monkeys. They were shooting at anything that moved in the high branches.

<They're killing everything!> Cassie cried, outraged. <We have to stop them!>

<This isn't time to play save-the-rain-forest, Cassie,> Marco snapped. <This is time to play save your own butt!>

<Jake!> Tobias yelled down from above. <I see Dracon beams being fired!>

<Yeah, we kind of noticed,> Rachel answered.

We had swung away from most of the slaughter. But we were still near enough to hear the wild, huffing laughter of the Hork-Bajir and the giddy, insane cries from the human-Controller.

I know there is a difference between human life and the lives of other animals. I mean, I *guess* there is. And I definitely know there is a difference between human life and the lives of trees. But still, that mindless, pointless massacre of trees and the animals in them made me sick.

The Hork-Bajir were just cutting everything down. Smouldering stumps stood where trees had been sliced up. The forest was screaming in anger and confusion.

HOO! HOOO! HOOHOOHOO!

Ke-RAW! Ke-RAW! Ke-RAW!

Then something strange happened.

As the Hork-Bajir stomped on through the

rain forest, something fell from a tree. It was very long, and it wrapped itself around the lead Hork-Bajir.

<A snake!> Rachel yelled.

<Man, I didn't know snakes came that big!> Marco said.

The snake swiftly coiled around the Hork-Bajir and squeezed. The other Hork-Bajir began to slash at it. Then. . .

<Get back, fools, and be glad I don't kill you all,> a sneering, thought-speak voice said.

The Hork-Bajir stopped trying to free their trapped friend very suddenly. They stepped back. And just watched the struggling Hork-Bajir.

I knew that thought-speak voice. We all did. Somehow the sound of it in your brain made you feel afraid.

Once the Hork-Bajir stopped struggling, the snake began to change. From the impossibly long snake body, an Andalite grew.

An Andalite body, at least. But not a true Andalite. Because in that Andalite head lived the Yeerk slug who held the rank of Visser Three.

It's strange, how two almost identical things can be so totally different. See, Visser Three looked almost exactly like Ax, or any other Andalite. And yet, there was never a moment of doubt when you saw him that this was an evil creature.

The four remaining Hork-Bajir and the

human-Controller were shaking with terror before the Visser.

<What are you fools doing?> the Visser asked in deceptively calm tones. He looked at the human-Controller.

Visser Three is never very careful about his thought-speak. Thought-speak is like E-mail: you can decide who it goes to. Or you can just blast it out for all to hear. I guess if you're as powerful as Visser Three, you just shout away.

The human-Controller turned several shades lighter than his natural colour. "We . . . we . . . we we we were following your orders, Visser. To destroy any animals that don't belong here because they could be the Andalite bandits."

<And you thought perhaps the trees were Andalites, as well?>

"No . . . it was . . . um. . ."

The Visser raked his Andalite tail forwards and pressed the blade against the man's throat. <Did it occur to you that the Bug fighter is less than a hundred metres from here? Did it occur to you that Dracon beams travel a long way? Did it occur to you that we cannot get back to our own time without that Bug fighter? And did it occur to you that I MIGHT BE IN MORPH and that you might end up shooting me?>

The human-Controller sank to his knees. "I didn't . . . we never . . . it . . . it . . . was them!" He pointed a finger of blame at the Hork-Bajir.

I whispered to Ax. <What's that about needing the Bug fighter to get back to his own time?>

Ax shrugged his monkey shoulders. <I don't know. I think . . . maybe we need to exactly recreate the intersection of the two Dracon beams to undo the *Sario Rip*. I remember something like that from school.> He held up the little disk from the Bug fighter's computer. <But they can't fly the Bug fighter without this.>

It came to me then, in a flash of insight: I had made a terrible mistake. I had risked Ax's life to get the computer, to make it impossible for the Yeerks to fly the Bug fighter. But now, we knew they'd have to fly the Bug fighter to get us home.

You could say we had a bargaining chip. You'd think maybe we could trade Visser Three the computer for a ride home. But I knew better. Once he had the computer, the Visser would just kill us.

We were trapped. Trapped, because of my own mistake.

Chapter 18

We had been in monkey morph for almost the two-hour limit. It was time to change and regroup, and hopefully figure out what to do next.

We swung away through the trees, far from Visser Three. We scampered down to the ground and began to demorph.

Tobias flew up and landed on a fallen tree beside us, since there were no low branches. There was a black, singed area on his tail.

"Tobias!" Cassie cried. She rushed over to him as soon as she was human again.

<I'm fine,> Tobias said, as Cassie lifted his tail to check for damage. <But someone took a shot at me and almost hit me. I guess one of the human-Controllers must have been a bird-watcher. He knew red-tails don't fly in the

122

Amazon. But before they chased me off, I saw them working on our crashed Bug fighter. Three Taxxons crawling all over it, repairing it. And a bunch of Hork-Bajir shooting anything they didn't like.>

I told Tobias what we'd overheard Visser Three saying. "They need the Bug fighter to get back to the right time. I don't know why, and Ax doesn't know why."

Ax was fully Andalite again. He held up the yellow disk. <They cannot fly that Bug fighter without this. I guarantee it.>

He was still focusing on that. Not thinking ahead to the fact that we needed the Yeerks to have the stupid computer now. I know it sounds weird, but I was actually mad at Ax for not seeing what an idiot I'd been. I wanted someone just to say, "Jake, you've blown it, man. You're not the leader any more."

It would have been a relief.

"Jake!" Rachel hissed.

"What?"

"Don't move. Don't anyone move a muscle," Rachel said.

I moved nothing but my eyes. From the bushes around us, utterly silent, the heads began to rise. Beside each head, a spear, cocked and ready to fly.

"I think the local guys have the drop on us," Marco said nervously.

I was amazed. It is impossible to sneak up on an Andalite. It is even more impossible to sneak up on a red-tailed hawk. And yet about twelve guys, some older, some younger, all with intense, jet-black eyes and black hair, had done just that.

There was no doubt in my mind that if we even twitched, let alone attacked, twelve poison-tipped spears would fly, and the six of us would go down permanently.

"Uh . . . Cassie?" Marco whispered. "You're the tree-hugging, save-the-rain-forest, love-the-planet person here. Who *are* these guys?"

"Humans," Cassie said.

"No duh," Marco said.

"That's all I know. Humans. Some bunch of people who live here. What am I, an encyclopaedia or something?"

"I don't think they like us," Rachel said. "But they don't look like they want to kill us."

I recognized one of the faces. It was the kid who'd thrown a spear at me before. His alert, black eyes watched me. Rachel was right: they didn't like us.

"I wonder if they saw us morph?" I decided to try raising my hands in a gesture of peace. Slowly, slowly, I raised my hands, palm out.

No one stabbed a spear in me. That was a good sign. I took a deep breath. Until that moment, I'd forgotten to breathe.

"Hello. We . . . um, we don't want any trouble," I said.

"You got that right," Marco whispered.

One of them stepped forward and came right up to face me. He may have been thirty or forty or eighty. I couldn't be sure. But he was definitely the leader of the group. You could tell.

He was wearing extremely little. So little I think Rachel and Cassie would have been embarrassed, if they weren't busy being terrified.

The man lowered his spear and peered intently into my face. He spoke. But it was no language I knew.

"Sorry, I don't speak, um, whatever."

The man thought that over for a moment. Then, he pointed a finger at me and said, "*Macaco*".

I guess when I didn't understand that, either, he decided I was an idiot. He launched into an amazingly good pantomime of a monkey.

"Oh, *monkey*? Monkey is *macaco*?"

The man nodded and smiled. Then the smile was gone. He jabbed a finger right in my chest. "*Macaco. Tu. Espírito macaco.*"

"Whoa!" Marco said. "That's Spanish. *Espíritu* means spirit or soul."

"Maybe it's Portuguese," Cassie said. "They speak Portuguese in Brazil. This man is probably the headman of his village. He probably has some dealings with the Brazilians. He must have learned some Portuguese."

"Portuguese, Spanish, they're sorta alike," Marco said. "Spanish is all my grandmother speaks. And my mother grew up speaking Spanish."

"So you can translate?" Rachel asked.

"Well, no. I mean, I know maybe fifty words. But it's easy to figure what he's saying. He's saying Jake is a monkey spirit. *Espírito macaco.*"

"So they did see us morph," I said. I nodded at the man. "Yes. *Espírito macaco.*" Yes, I was a monkey spirit.

He looked hard at Ax. At his extra stalk eyes and his wicked tail. "*Mal. Diabo.*"

"I'm guessing he's calling Ax a devil," Marco said.

I shook my head firmly. "No *mal*. No *diabo*."

The man glared at Ax. Then he took the butt of his short spear and began to draw something in the dirt. It took a few seconds for me to recognize it. It was a creature with two arms, two legs, and a tail. It had blades on its elbows, knees, and head. The man pointed at the drawing. "*Diabo. Monstro.*"

I swear I almost started laughing in sheer relief. The man had drawn a Hork-Bajir. "Yes, definitely. *Mal. Diabo. Monstro* and any other bad word you can think of."

I took my bare foot and rubbed out the drawing.

"He liked that," Rachel said.

The guy grinned and slapped his chest. "Polo."

"That's either his name or his favourite brand of shirt," Marco said.

I pointed at myself and said, "Jake."

The man nodded. Then he rubbed out what was left of the Hork-Bajir picture. He grinned a huge grin. He laughed out loud, and all his men and boys laughed with him. Even the kid who'd tried to shish kebab me.

"You know, I think I like these guys," Rachel said.

Suddenly, the skies opened up, and rain came pouring down on us. Pouring down like we were standing under Niagara Falls.

Polo grabbed my hand and forearm in a strong grip. We were sealing a deal.

"*Diabos. Matar diabos.*"

"I think he said hunt . . . kill the devils," Marco said.

I looked into Polo's eyes. I had no doubts. "That is exactly what he said."

Polo and his people stepped back into the bushes, and in an instant they were invisible in the pouring rain.

"Those little guys up against Hork-Bajir warriors?" Rachel shook her head sceptically.

"I have a feeling about those 'little guys'," Cassie said. "I think maybe this forest is theirs, and they don't like a bunch of alien *diabos* stomping around killing everything in sight."

"Better to have them on our side than against us, that's for sure," I said.

Suddenly I felt really tired. Too many dangers. Too much adrenaline. And even though it was just late afternoon here, in Brazil, in this time, my own body had been awake and fighting and morphing for almost twenty-four hours.

The rain was just absolutely pouring down from the sky. Tobias couldn't even think about flying. I could see I wasn't the only one exhausted.

"So this would be the 'rain' part of rain forest," Marco said. "They don't do anything halfway around here, do they?"

We trudged through the downpour, drinking our fill from the water that drained down off the leaves.

But finally, I saw that no one could go any farther. At least I couldn't. Time was running out — we had just about three hours. We had no solid plan. It was the worst possible time for a rest. But there was no going on. Not yet.

"Let's take a break," I said.

"Where?" Marco asked.

I flopped down in the mud and rested my back against a tree. "Right here, man. Right here."

Cassie came and sat beside me. The noise of the falling rain made our conversation private.

"How are you doing?" Cassie asked me.

I shrugged. "I'm fine. Why wouldn't I be?"

She looked at me sceptically. "Jake, I know you. I can see it on your face. You're worried. And you're mad. Since I don't think you're mad at any of us, I'm guessing you're mad at yourself."

I looked away. "Everything will work out," I lied dully.

"You know, it was kind of funny seeing you and Polo together."

"Yeah? Why?" I didn't really care. I was too tired to care. But Cassie was being kind, and I needed some kindness.

"Because you're the same, you and Polo. He's you, and you're him. The leaders. You know, he took a risk putting down his spear. We might have killed him and his people. There was no way he could know if it was the right thing to do. He just made the best decision he could. That's all anyone can ask from any leader."

I felt for Cassie's hand in the rain. It was too dim and grey to see her face well.

"I'm so tired," I said.

Cassie laid her head on my shoulder. "I know, Jake. Rest. Just rest."

Chapter 19

6:49 P.M.

I woke up suddenly, with the feeling that I had slept too long.

I opened my eyes.

Black night. Night so black it was like being smothered in black felt.

But not everything was dark.

Fifteen centimetres away from my face, two eyes glowed green and gold. I could smell foul breath. I could *feel* its breath on my face.

Jaguar!

The big cat stuck its nose closer to me, trying to decide who I was, and what I was doing in its forest.

I might have wet my pants right then from sheer terror. I don't know, because I was soaked to the bone from the rain, which had finally ended. I was sitting in mud, feeling the adrenaline pump into my veins. Feeling fear again.

I was going to live or die depending on what the jaguar decided. Was I food? Or was I not? If the cat was hungry, and if I smelled like prey, it would sink its massive yellow fangs into my neck and it would all be over in a second.

I wouldn't even get the chance to scream.

Then, a faint memory of hope! There was one thing I could do. No time to morph, but. . .

As slowly as I could, I raised a trembling hand to touch the jaguar's spotted fur. I focused my mind. I concentrated fervently on acquiring the jaguar. And I prayed the jaguar would act like most animals act when they are acquired. I hoped it would go into a trance.

When I opened my eyes, the jaguar closed his.

"Marco!" I hissed. "Cassie! Rachel! Ax! Tobias! Somebody!"

"Wha? Huh?" Marco said groggily. Then, "Whoa! Whoa! Wake up, you guys! Jeez, Jake, what are you doing? That jaguar could chomp you."

"Really? I hadn't thought about that, Marco. Thanks for pointing that out to me. Now, look, I'm acquiring him to keep him calm. Here's what we do. One after another, we acquire him, then we move off. Ax?"

<Yes, Prince Jake,> Ax said.

"You think you can outrun this big kitty?"

131

<Yes.>

"OK, then Ax, you acquire him last, and run for it. Just in case he's in a bad mood."

Five minutes later, we were all a safe distance away.

"You know, you were probably fairly safe, Jake," Cassie said. "I doubt jaguars eat prey your size."

<I'll bet they eat prey *my* size,> Tobias muttered.

"What's cool is we all have a jaguar morph now. Perfect for travelling in the rain forest at night," Cassie pointed out.

"Speaking of which, it's late," Rachel said. "Ticktock."

<We have two of your hours left,> Ax said.

"Two hours to find the Blade ship, smuggle aboard, and hope Visser Three knows how to get us all back to our normal time," Rachel said. "Wonderful."

"The jaguars are predators," Cassie pointed out. "That means senses adapted for hunting in the rain forest. They would be able to find the Yeerks, if any animal could."

Marco laughed. "Cassie, you're just looking for an excuse to morph something new."

"Cassie's right," I said. "Look how dark it is. I can't even see you guys. No streetlights, no house lights, no car lights, even moonlight and starlight can't penetrate the trees. We're helpless in this dark. Barefoot, lost and blind. We need eyes. We can morph owls, but we don't know what dangers the rain forest might hold for a plain old horned owl. Jaguars, on the other hand, look like they can take care of themselves."

"Let's do it," Rachel said. "We're totally helpless in this darkness."

"We need a way to carry the Bug fighter's computer with us," Cassie pointed out. She tore a strip of cloth from her shirt-tail, twisted it, and threaded it through a small hole in the computer core.

"I'll take it," I said. The computer was my stupid mistake. I should carry it. Cassie slipped it over my head. It hung like a big, dorky medallion.

I took a deep breath. "OK, boys and girls and Andalites. Let's morph."

<Jake, I have to try to fly up above the trees, try to get some moonlight,> Tobias said. <I'm as blind as you guys are down here.>

The jaguar was a strange morph for one reason: because it wasn't strange at all. It was just like morphing the tiger. The jaguar is smaller and stockier than a tiger. But it is still one of the big cats.

But for the others, it was their first experience with a big cat. As my jaguar eyes came on and the darkness grew much lighter, I could see the final transformations.

I saw the long, yellowed teeth grow in Cassie's mouth. I saw the pattern of large, hollow spots spread across Rachel's skin. I saw the claws sprout from Ax's weak Andalite hands. I saw the way Marco fell forwards to land on all fours as his tail extended like a snake behind him.

<Oh, this is beautiful,> Marco said. <Oh, man! Oh, man! Feel the rush!>

<Hah-hah!> Rachel crowed. <This is like, so alive! It's so not afraid!>

I knew the feeling. It's different being an animal at the top of the food chain. An animal that doesn't worry much about being killed. It's not arrogance, really. It's an absence of fear. Just like a tiger, a jaguar may be startled, surprised, alarmed, but never afraid. It may run away in the face of humans or loud machinery, for example, but somehow it isn't afraid when it does that.

I saw Rachel take a swipe at the air, testing the speed of her paws. <Not as powerful as a grizzly bear, but awfully fast.>

<Excellent senses,> Cassie said. <I smell . . . wow. I smell about a million things.>

<I'm having a strange desire to eat a monkey,> Marco said. <And yet, I was a monkey a few hours ago. We're all going to end up in the nuthouse someday. You realize that, right?>

<Tobias? Can you hear me?> I called in thought-speak.

<Yeah, I hear you. It's much better up here. There's a three-quarter moon and a million stars! I can see well enough to fly, but I'd break my neck if I tried to land.>

<There are far more than a million stars,> Ax commented.

<I know, Ax-man,> Tobias said with a laugh. <Hey! Hey! There's a glow. Like a town, maybe. Lots of lights.>

<If they're still working on the Blade ship, they'd have lights, right?> Cassie pointed out.

<It's the only clue we have, and we are running out of time,> I said. <Let's go.>

<Go into the light,> Marco said.

<What?>

<*Poltergeist*. That old movie. Don't you remember? The little munchkin lady saying, 'Go into the light, go into the light'?>

<What was this light?> Ax asked, completely mystified.

<I think it was like . . . death, or something,> Marco said. <But, hey, I could be wrong. Maybe it was just a big, bright, afterlife McDonald's.>

<Shut up, Marco,> Rachel said.

We had two hours left. Then, if Ax was right, the *Sario Rip* would end, and the universe would have two Jakes and two Cassies, and would eliminate them both.

Go to the Blade ship. Get aboard. Hope

Visser Three could get us back. Somehow. Even without the Bug fighter's computer.

Not much of a plan. But I was the leader, and a leader has to give people hope. Even when he doesn't have much himself.

<Let's go and see what this light is,> I said.

Chapter 20

6:05 P.M.

Even through the eyes of the jaguar, the rain forest was dark.

But, oh, the things I saw, gliding like a ghost along the jungle floor.

It was like some incredible theme park ride. Like one of those haunted houses, where each turn of the little car you're in brings you face-to-face with a new goblin or ghoul or skeleton.

But it wasn't dead spirits that I saw in my trip through the rain forest. It was life. Life in more shapes and types than you can imagine.

Huge snakes, seven metres long and as big around as the branches they hung from. And snakes so tiny they could almost have been worms.

Monstrous insects, beetles the size of your

fist, and centipedes as big as rats. And rats as big as poodles. At least, they looked like rats. And frogs in bright, warning, touch-me-and-die colours.

And ants everywhere, some marching along in columns, with each ant carrying a piece of leaf ten times its own size. Lizards that shot past, flashes of green. And what I assume were salamanders, like lizards but in brilliant, slimy colours. And overhead, birds and monkeys and more birds.

We had been blind as bats, stomping through the rain forest in our human bodies. We had seen nothing. But the jaguar saw and smelled and heard everything.

A million species of life filled the forest around us. Forms of life stranger than anything that had come from outer space. Incredible, insane, brilliant life, all fighting to stay alive, all working to grab one little piece of the rain forest.

It was overwhelming. For a long time, none of us said anything. We were discovering a world we had never even guessed at. It was as if Polo and his people had been transported to a shopping mall at Christmas-time. They would have been amazed and stunned at all the things man creates.

Now, the reverse was happening. This was the world the jaguar knew. And it was the world that

Polo and his people knew. Their shopping mall at Christmas-time, filled, not with all the things man makes, but with all the wild, amazing, insane, extreme, shocking creativity of nature.

And every time I thought, *Well, I've seen it all*, the rain forest would answer, Kid, you haven't seen anything. Take a look at *this* bird! Take a look at *that* flower! Get a load of *this* creature! Little human boy, I have more to show you than you could see in ten lifetimes.

<OK,> Rachel said, breaking the silence at last. <I take it back. I don't want to pave over the rain forest. I don't care if it is dangerous and deadly and it's trying to kill us.>

<You have an amazing planet,> Ax said. <Amazing.>

Surprisingly, it was Cassie who reminded us of our mission. <We have very little time left. We have to get to the Blade ship.>

<You're right, Cassie, but I thought you'd be enjoying this,> I said. <This is the ultimate nature walk.>

<Yes, it is,> she said softly. <And the Yeerks want to destroy it, and anything else they can't use on this planet. I'm not going to let that happen. So let's haul butt, find the Blade ship, get back where we should be, stay alive to keep fighting, because *no one*, man or alien, is messing this place up while I'm around to stop them.>

<Yes, ma'am,> I said.

<I see lights up ahead,> Marco said.

From high above us: <I'm over the lights now. It's not a village. It's the Blade ship. And guess what? They dragged the Bug fighter here, too.>

Something about that fact . . . that the Bug fighter was with the Blade ship, made me uneasy.

There was no reason for Visser Three to have his people drag the two ships together. There was something wrong there. Something I should see. Something I should realize.

But I shook it off. My problem was that I needed a plan. It was time to think, not time to worry about things that made no sense.

Chapter 21

We crept, silent as a dream, through the bush. One foot in front of the other, sliding through leaves, our jaguar spots confusing to the eye, invisible.

The Hork-Bajir had chopped down a clearing around the Blade ship. There were Taxxons crawling over and around the ship, working feverishly. The Taxxons appeared to have finished work on the Bug fighter. Taxxons are like gigantic centipedes with raw, red circular mouths at one end, and a ring of eyes like red jelly.

<They fit right in,> Marco said.

I was thinking the same thing. The Taxxons could be rain forest natives. Although, even by rain forest standards, they would have been huge.

<Not enough Hork-Bajir,> Ax said. <There

should be more. Many more. They should be ringing the perimeter.>

<I count just five Hork-Bajir,> Rachel said. <Wait! Look! Inside the Blade ship. Through that window. Visser Three.>

I stared hard and saw the outline of an Andalite head. <Yeah. Good. At least we know where he is.>

<What do we do?> Rachel asked.

She was asking me. And I didn't happen to have any brilliant answers.

<OK, we know Visser Three needs the Bug fighter to get back to our time, right? And we have the computer core, so he can't use the Bug fighter without us. So . . . we could bargain with him, but he can't be trusted. Or we could sneak aboard the Blade ship and just leave the computer core where he can find it.>

<If he just happens to find the computer core lying around, he's going to know how it got there. And he's going to know what we're up to,> Marco said.

<Time is running out,> Ax said.

<If we stow away on the Blade ship but don't give Visser Three the computer core, we're trapped here, along with him,> Cassie pointed out.

I felt like my head was swimming. Somehow I'd just hoped there would be an answer at the end. But there wasn't.

<Look, I don't know, all right?!> I yelled. <I

don't know. I don't know what to do. I don't have any magic answer.>

<Jake, you're supposed to be our fearless leader,> Marco said.

I swear, I almost lost it right then. If we'd both been in human form, I might have punched Marco.

<I never said I was anyone's leader! I never asked to lead anything. Why do I have to know the answers? You don't, Marco. You don't, Rachel.>

<Oh, man,> Marco groaned. <Jake, you can't lose it, man. We need you.>

I was about to say something very rude when Cassie interrupted. <Something has been bothering me. Why is Jake the only one who had those flashes? We all exist in both places at once, right? So why is he the only one who had jungle hallucinations?>

The question hit me like a sledgehammer. Of course. It made no sense. I should have seen it. Should have, should have, should have! There were too many should haves!

Ax! I remembered asking him if there was some other way to get back. I remembered the way he avoided answering. <Ax? What do you know that you're not saying?>

<What do I *know*?> he answered evasively.

<What do you know . . . or *guess*?>

<Prince Jake, as I said, I know very little about *Sario Rips*. I was preoccupied by—>

<Ax. You call me your prince. Fine, I'm your prince. So answer my question.>

<Prince Jake . . . it's possible that you are . . . I mean, it's possible that you are the only real person here. The rest of us may only be memory.>

I felt a chill. <What are you talking about?>

<We may not actually be here. Not really. I mean, yes, we were here in one time line, but that time line was later erased.>

<Erased? Who erased this time line?>

<You, Prince Jake. It is possible that only you will escape from this time line. You may go back, alone, and alter everything, so that none of this ever really happens.>

<Is it just me, or is this truly insane?> Marco asked.

<Ax, how would I be the only one to escape this time line? We think the way to get back to our own time involves repeating the Dracon beam accident that caused the *Sario Rip*. Right?>

<Maybe . . . Prince Jake, that may not be the only way,> Ax said. <There may be *another* way. I didn't want to say anything because I wasn't sure. And—>

<Hey!> Tobias interrupted sharply. <Visser Three in the window over there? I just saw him wobble. Like a TV picture with interference. It's not him! It's a projection!>

<A decoy!> Rachel said.

x

144

Suddenly, I saw my terrible mistake. Visser Three knew that eight fifty-four was the cut-off. He knew. And he figured we knew, too.

So he knew that we'd show up, either at the Bug fighter or the Blade ship, trying to beat that deadline. He knew we'd try to hide out aboard one of the two ships. That's why he had his creatures drag the Bug fighter through the forest to be alongside the Blade ship.

So we'd have only one place to go.

So he'd know exactly where we'd be before eight fifty-four.

<It's a trap!> I yelled. <It's a trap! He's expecting us!>

And at that very moment, we heard his voice in our heads.

<Five cats and a bird. Hah-hah-hah. This will be too easy.>

Chapter 22

8:00 P.M.

<Run! It's a trap!>

I bolted. But a vine reached up and snagged my front paws. I tumbled, head over heels. Instantly the jaguar was up, but again a vine grabbed me, wrapping around my neck.

The vines were alive!

Like a snake, it wrapped around my jaguar throat and tightened. I couldn't breathe! I writhed with all the jaguar's strength and broke free.

I ran, then . . . it hit me! I'd been wearing the Bug fighter's computer around my neck. It was gone!

<It's a *Lerdethak*!> Ax yelled. <The vines! It's Visser Three in a morph. It's a creature from the Hork-Bajir home world: a *Lerdethak*. It—>

146

Suddenly Ax was silent.

The darkness was erupting around me in a tangle of vines. It was like being in a storm of snakes. The vines shot through the air, reaching, grabbing, wrapping themselves around me.

I saw a flash of a jaguar — maybe Ax, I couldn't be sure — being lifted in the air by one of the living vines. Lifted by his neck, with three more vines wrapping around his legs and body.

I wanted to help, but the snake-like things were everywhere! If I hesitated even a second, they would have me.

<Jake!> I heard Marco yell. <It's got me!>

Cassie's thought-speak voice just screamed. <Aaaaahhhh!>

<Cassie!> I yelled. <Marco!>

<Jake! It's huge!> Tobias yelled down from above. <Can't see well, but like a . . . like an octopus but with a thousand tentacles!>

A slither of tentacles slapped against me, wrapping around my legs. I leaped . . . a split second away from being caught.

I ran. What else could I do? I ran!

<It's swallowing them!> Tobias cried. <Oh, no! NO! It has a mouth. Huge! Help them!>

<I can't! I can't!> I cried.

The vine-tentacles were less numerous now, smaller, weaker.

<I'm inside something!> Rachel said. <Smothering!>

147

<Prince Jake, we've been swallowed by the *Lerdethak*!>

<I can't get to you!> I yelled. <I can't even see you! Claw your way out!>

<Can't . . . can't move. . .> Cassie moaned.

<I can't just watch this!> Tobias yelled. <I'm going down!>

I was reeling from sheer shock and horror. I was running in panic, running flat out. The tentacles no longer surrounded me. But when I paused, panting, to look back, I saw it.

It was like some gnarled old tree come to life. Like Medusa's head, alive with snakes. I saw it outlined against the bright lights around the Blade ship. It was rising from the ground, growing taller and taller. Tentacles like bull-whips! A maze of snake-like arms, all surrounding a dark core. Through the tentacles I could see a wide, drooping, blue-outlined mouth.

As I watched, a struggling jaguar was tossed inside.

And one thin tentacle reached, whipped, and wrapped around a bird that was diving towards it.

<Hmmm,> Visser Three said. <Just five little Andalites inside my craw. That leaves one still free. But don't worry. Plenty of time to find you.>

He had them all. He had them all but me.

<Settle down, my Andalite friends. Relax. I won't kill you, yet. But you won't morph your

148

way out of this. My *Lerdethak* morph will hold you tight till I decide your fates.>

He had them. Visser Three had won. I was the only one left. I was their only hope.

Some hope, I told myself bitterly. I was the one in charge. And I had walked them into Visser Three's trap. *Don't feel sorry for yourself, Jake. Find a way out!*

The huge, thousand-tentacled creature moved easily and swiftly through the rain forest. And now, on both sides of it, I saw the Hork-Bajir warriors.

Behind me! All around me! A ring of Hork-Bajir penning me in as Visser Three slithered towards me.

Then. . .

FLIT!

Even my jaguar eyes couldn't see the spear fly. I could only see it when it stuck into the back of a Hork-Bajir.

FLIT! FLIT! FLIT!

Spears appeared from nowhere. Hork-Bajir began dropping!

Polo stepped into view. He looked past me and launched his spear at the *Lerdethak*. Launched it at Visser Three.

But the Visser's morph was far too quick. One vine reached out, snatched the spear from the air, and contemptuously tossed it back. It stuck in the ground where Polo grabbed it.

There was no way to stop the *Lerdethak*. It was safe, surrounded by its vine-tentacles. The only vulnerable part was the head, and it was surrounded by a forest of the —

Wait a minute!

Not like vines! Not like tentacles! *Wrong way to think, Jake,* I realized. *Branches. Like branches!*

I dived into darkness and even as I ran, I began to demorph. I heard the flit of spears flying and the cries of Hork-Bajir. But nothing was stopping the *Lerdethak*.

The Visser kept coming.

I was human now, blundering blindly through slapping leaves, my bare feet cut and bruised. But at least I had a plan. I ran and focused on a quick morph. I ran and shrank, but still I ran, even as my legs became bowed and I bent forward to use my knuckles like extra feet.

And when I was fully monkey . . . I turned.

The *Lerdethak* loomed huge above me. Its thousand bullwhip tentacles slashed the air.

<Is that you, my last Andalite?> Visser Three crowed. <Is that little creature your final morph? Pathetic.>

Maybe so, I thought. *But as far as I'm concerned, you're just one big jungle gym.*

I leaped through the air.

Leaped for the nearest tentacle.

I grabbed it, swung, and flew!

No other animal could have penetrated that maze of swinging, snapping, slithering tentacles. But to the monkey, it was all vines and branches.

Swing! Fly! Catch! Swing! Fly! Catch!

All at hyperspeed! All at warp factor ten! But the monkey could do it!

I grabbed one especially big tentacle. It swung me far up in the air, trying to snap me loose. But I held on. And now, down below, I could see the *Lerdethak's* head. I could see the drooping blue mouth that had just swallowed the others.

I glanced aside. Polo! Yes, he was standing with his spear in his hand.

<Your spear!> I cried in thought-speak. <Your spear!>

In a flash, Polo understood. He threw with all his might.

The spear flew straight and true.

And from high in the air, holding to the whipping tentacle with my tail alone, I reached with both hands and snatched the spear out of the air.

Did you know that one of the reasons humans can throw is because we once swung through the trees? Yep. The shoulder design that makes it possible to swing from branch to branch makes it possible to throw a spear.

Very possible.

I threw.

151

The spear hit home! It sank into the flesh of the *Lerdethak*, delivering the poisons of the rain forest into the deadly alien creature.

But I had used up all my luck.

A tentacle whipped towards me. Like a snapped high-tension wire, it wrapped itself around my neck, and —

Chapter 23

—I misjudged the distance to the ground, hit it too hard, and rolled over, a tangle of wings and talons.

<Nice landing,> Tobias said with a laugh.

"Are you OK?" Cassie asked me. She rushed over and picked me up. Then she set me back down because I was starting to demorph. And I was getting heavier pretty quickly.

"What the. . ." I demanded. I almost had a heart attack. I was back! Back, behind the motel. Back, getting ready to go to the Safeway.

Was it a flashback? One of the visions?

No, it was lasting too long. This was real. I was behind the motel. Getting ready to morph and go check out the Safeway.

I looked at my watch. Could it be? "What

153

time is it?" I asked Ax.

<Eight-nineteen,> he said.

Eight-nineteen. Of course. I knew the time. At eight-nineteen, I had felt strange — uneasy about making the decision to go into the supermarket. But I had made the decision to go ahead. And from that decision, everything else had followed. The *Sario Rip*. The disaster in the rain forest.

"Cassie? Have you ever been to the Amazon?" I asked.

"What? No. Of course not," she said.

It hadn't happened. At least not to this Cassie. It was still something that was going to happen. Unless I changed the time line.

"Are we doing this or what?" Rachel demanded impatiently. "Come on, Jake, are we doing this or what?"

I grinned. I laughed. I'm afraid I flat out giggled. "Or what, Rachel. Definitely 'or what'. We are out of here!"

It was a day later before I finally got a chance to talk to Ax alone. I told him everything. He thought I was nuts until I said the words *Sario Rip*. Then he knew.

<This is all very amazing,> he said as we walked through the woods. The good old, familiar woods. The woods without killer ants and piranhas and jaguars and snakes and natives with

poison spears. <I have no memory of any of this.>

"Yeah, it was pretty amazing," I said. "I made so many wrong moves, I screwed everything up. The computer . . . letting us walk into a trap. . . I mean, we were pretty much doomed. Then it was like I got a second chance to keep it from happening. But I don't even know how. You . . . I mean, that other you, or however you want to say it, thought we had to recreate the *Sario Rip* in order to undo it."

Ax nodded. <Yes, I suppose that would have worked. And there was only one other way.>

I stopped him. "You never told me about any other way."

<No, I wouldn't have,> Ax said. <I don't know it for sure . . . but there is a theory.>

"I thought there might be," I said drily.

<It is impossible for one person to be in two places at once. In theory. So if you . . . eliminate . . . one of the two, well, the consciousness snaps back together. I think what happened, Prince Jake, is that you died.>

I felt a chill run up my spine.

<But even as you died in the rain forest, you were still alive here. So your mind snapped back. Then you undid the time line, so none of it ever really happened. You would find you cannot morph the jaguar or the monkey, because you never really acquired those animals.>

He made an Andalite smile, which just

involves the eyes, since they have no mouths.

"They teach this stuff in your schools, huh?"

<Yes.>

"And you didn't pay much attention to this lesson, huh?"

<True.>

"I can see why," I said. "This time travel stuff will make your head explode."

<Exactly,> Ax agreed. <And on that day, there was this game . . . and this female. . .>

We walked a while further. "It was a disaster down there, Ax. I blew it. The only reason we're all still alive is that in the end, I got lucky."

<Maybe that is true, Prince Jake. But my brother Elfangor once told me, "It's a leader's job to be lucky". Sometimes, success is just luck.>

I nodded. It didn't make me feel any better. "Elfangor's luck ran out."

<Yes. We must hope yours does not, Prince Jake.>

I laughed. "Don't call me 'Prince'."

<Yes, Prince Jake.>